THE MAIL ORDER BRIDE'S PROMISE

SHADY FORKS BRIDES

BLYTHE CARVER

1

———

Aileen Riley sat in the room as her family played cards at a table a few feet from where she was doing embroidery. Her legs were perched on the couch next to her, and she was relaxed on the armrest, leaning toward the glowing lantern.

She looked up from her needlework when Theresa laughed. Theresa Winchester was across from her husband, Nate, and the two were playing cards with Rich and Annie Winchester. Rich and Nate were brothers. Aileen had been a companion to Theresa before her marriage to Nate and came along with her when she moved from Boston to Shady Forks, Wyoming.

And here she had stayed for the last four years, becoming a nanny for the children of the Winchester family. She loved her job and loved them all like family, even though they weren't blood related. She'd come from the poor side of Boston and was hired by Theresa's parents to be the family maid. It was their journey westward which led her to be Theresa's companion, and now the family's nanny

.

They treated her like she was a member of the family. That's why she'd stayed for so long.

She set the embroidery down and listened to their chatter, moving her green eyes from one to another, feeling different levels of affection for each one. She admired Annie's bright spirit. Nate took care of Theresa well, and since Theresa was like a sister to Aileen, she appreciated and respected him for it. Nate's brother Rich was just as much a gentleman as Nate, earning her respect quickly and keeping it through the years.

As much as she loved the people she considered family, Aileen had been itching for something new. Her thirtieth birthday was in two weeks. She had no children of her own. She'd never been in love. The only thing she remembered before joining Theresa's family in Boston as an employee was hardship and struggle.

She was sure this wasn't all there was to life. God hadn't put her on this earth to make no mark. She wanted to leave a legacy of some kind. Children were that legacy.

There was no prospect of marriage in Shady Forks. That was something Aileen knew for a fact.

"Aileen, what *are* you thinking about?" Theresa brought her out of her thoughts, the innocent question spoken in an amused voice.

Aileen looked at her friend. "I'm thinking about how old I'm getting."

Theresa lifted her eyebrows. "That's why you have such a god-awful look on your face. My goodness, Aileen. You're only turning thirty. And I told you we wouldn't throw a surprise party for you. You already know about the party. It's hardly a surprise now."

All four of them were smiling at her, making it impossible for her not to smile back.

"Yes, I know," she said, nodding. "I know about the party. I appreciate it very much. I'm just feeling a little restless, is all."

"There's nothing wrong with that," Nate said. "I

find that feeling to be really motivational when I'm trying to get work done at my shop."

"I haven't found a way to put it to good use yet," Aileen responded, turning her smile to him.

"Well, if you think of anything," Theresa said firmly, "you better come and tell me. I'll make sure you're able to do whatever it is you want to do."

Aileen thanked her, and the group went back to their game when Annie made a slick move and managed to beat them all at that hand.

"I was distracted," Nate cried out, throwing his hands up in the air.

His brother laughed. "I was, too."

"I thought winning was the name of the game," Annie said innocently, widening her eyes and blinking at the three of them.

This made them all laugh. Nate leaned forward and swept all the cards together into a pile in the middle of the table. He began to sort them and straighten them until it was time to shuffle.

Aileen watched them go back to their game, aware that Theresa had brought her into the conversation so she wouldn't feel alone. Like the odd man out. The way Melissa, Nate and Rich's sister, must have felt before she got married and moved on with her husband.

The gesture was appreciated. But it didn't change things. She was still the only one left who didn't have a beau, a husband, or even a suitor. She was alone, and she didn't want to be.

There was only one way to change that. Aileen knew of a way to make the change she sought. Four years ago, Theresa had answered a mail-order bride ad from Nate to come to Wyoming and be his bride to help him take care of his two sons after the death of his wife.

As much as she didn't want to leave, Aileen knew it was time. She'd been thinking about it long enough. Tomorrow would be the day for her. She would go to Shady Forks newsstand and get the Matrimonial Times and a newspaper from the nearest cities. Usually, the men in those ads were asking for women from the east. But she didn't see how that would make a difference. If he was seeking a wife, he ought to be preferring one who already knew what life in the west was like.

Aileen was accustomed to the climate and the way of life. She preferred Wyoming over Boston now and had no plans to return there.

When she slipped between the covers that night, Aileen was excited. She could feel it. The adventure was coming. There would finally be a reason for her to get up in the morning. There would be something to look forward to, different things than she was used to—different people.

It would be a welcome change.

2

The sun was almost too bright for Aileen when she stepped out of the house the next morning. The children were all in school, with the exception of the baby, who was with her mother, Theresa. Theresa was a proud new mother. She adored being a stepmother, but Aileen saw a real difference in her friend now that she was the mother of her own child.

She lifted one hand to shade her eyes and walked toward the barn. She'd told Derek of her intentions before breakfast and asked him to have her horse ready. She didn't see him anywhere, there was no horse waiting for her, and the door to the stable was closed.

She opened the door that was sized for humans

instead of pulling the large one open. As soon as she went in, she saw Derek standing in the aisle between the stalls, adjusting the saddle on Ironwood, her horse.

"Oh, Derek, thank you. I thought you might have forgotten."

Derek smiled at her, pulling the horse by the reins and handing them to her. "Of course not, Miss Aileen. You only told me a few hours ago. I wouldn't forget that quickly."

Aileen didn't know why she felt that way. She was sure it was something she was telling herself—that no one was noticing her, that she was easily forgotten. These things weren't true. She tried telling herself that, too, and had yet to be convincing enough to keep the thoughts away.

Truth be told, Aileen felt like she was empty, a waste of space, doing nothing with her life, accomplishing nothing. She was good with the children and was a proper nanny. But those weren't *her* children. And even if they remembered her, they wouldn't the way a child remembers his or her mother.

She thanked Derek again and walked outside, with Ironwood following behind her dutifully. Once outside, Derek helped her into the saddle, and she rode off toward town, pulling out her parasol and putting it over her head. It was such a sunny day. There wasn't a cloud in the Wyoming sky.

The newspaper stand was across from the community building. Sometimes, Aileen had sat there, watching the people come and go, wondering what they were doing there. They had business. They were taking care of errands. They were useful.

Aileen was determined to find someone to be useful for, too. Theresa had found her man. When would it be her turn?

She left her horse in front of the community building, in the lot where people left their buggies and horses when they had business there. She walked across to the newspaper stand and bought the *Matrimonial Times* and two newspapers from Wyoming cities.

She would have preferred if no one knew what she was doing until she was ready to tell people. But she knew by the look on Max's face when she purchased the magazine that he'd immediately caught on. She slipped away from the stand as fast as she could to avoid any questions, giving him a polite smile and dashing away as if she had a lot to do.

There was a spot on a hill nearby that was part of the church grounds. Aileen had often gone there to sit on pretty days, do some sewing, write a poem, try to draw a sketch, and failing miserably. She thought it was the most beautiful place in Shady Forks.

That was where she was headed. She'd brought a blanket with her and retrieved it from the saddle-bags on Ironwood's back before heading for her spot on foot.

Her heart sank when she saw there was someone else under the tree. The young woman had brought her own blanket and was sitting on it, leaning back against the tree, a book on her lap. It almost looked like she was sleeping, and then she lifted one knee and tilted her head back, bringing the book up to eye level.

Aileen passed through the small white gate and headed up the path anyway, determined to enjoy her tree in her spot, even if there was someone else there enjoying it, too.

She came closer and recognized Heidi Schnei-der, the mayor's daughter. She was a quiet girl, as far as Aileen knew, never caused any trouble, and could often be seen walking around Shady Forks with her nose in a book.

"Good morning," the girl said, looking up at Aileen as she approached.

"Good morning, Heidi. How are you today?"

"I'm feeling well. Just out enjoying the sun. I guess you had the same idea, didn't you?"

Aileen nodded, glancing down at the magazines in her arms. She didn't mind if Heidi knew about her plans before others did. She was confident the young girl wouldn't say anything to anyone. She wasn't known for spreading gossip—whether true or not. She stayed out of business that wasn't hers.

She did notice, however, when Heidi's eyes dropped to the magazines, and they widened just a bit.

"Are you making plans, Aileen?" she asked in an interested voice.

Aileen looked down once more. She could feel her cheeks warm. "I... I am, yes."

"That is very interesting," the girl breathed, setting her book aside after dog-earring the page where she'd left off. She turned to Aileen, an excited look on her face. "Can I ask you some questions about it?"

Aileen spread her blanket out on the grass near Heidi and sat down. "What can I tell you? I haven't done it yet."

"No, but that's how Mrs. Winchester met Mr. Winchester, right? *Your* Mrs. Winchester. Not the other one. Annie. You know what I mean."

Aileen laughed, nodding. "Yes, one too many Mrs. Winchesters, right?"

Heidi giggled. "And Mr. Winchesters. I'd rather just call them by their first names, but Pa says that's not very respectful. I don't want anyone getting upset with me."

"Well, while we're talking, you can just call them by their first names. What do you say?"

Heidi gave her a grateful look. "Thank you. Anyway, that is how Theresa got here, right?"

Aileen nodded. "Yes, that's right. I'm planning on finding a husband this way. It was so successful for her. I've waited long enough, I think."

Heidi tilted her head to the side. "I know you will make some man very happy, Aileen. You're so pretty and nice."

Aileen giggled, a tingle of affection sweeping through her body. "Well, thank you, Heidi. That's awfully sweet of you to say. I didn't think people really had an opinion of me."

"What?" The girl looked genuinely surprised, pulling back slightly. "Why, that's ridiculous. We love you here in Shady Forks. You should know that. Even my pa speaks very highly of you."

Aileen laughed out loud. "Even? Does he speak ill of other people?"

"No, he just doesn't give an opinion at all," Heidi responded. "He is the mayor, you know. He's supposed to be representing everyone. Looking at things from different points of view and taking in all perspectives. He talks about that all the time. So he doesn't voice opinions much, especially about people. If he's saying nice things about you, that's an accomplishment."

"Well, that's very flattering," Aileen responded. "Thank you for telling me."

"Of course. I think it's something you should know if you plan to leave Shady Forks and seek out a husband and family somewhere else. I'm sure they will love you, Aileen. You are easy to love."

"My goodness, I'm so happy you came up here to the oak tree today, Heidi. You've really made me feel a whole lot better."

Heidi nodded. "It's always nice to be encouraged." She sighed dramatically, letting her shoulders slouch. "We will miss you, though, so terribly. We really will."

Aileen just smiled at the girl, feeling a little teary-eyed.

3

Donald Ferris carefully drew the needle through the leather. Even though he was concentrating hard on what he was doing, his mind was elsewhere.

He'd been living in Gustaf's Corner for a long time. He'd spent the better part of his life on the McArthur ranch, working as the second in command for an elderly man. The foreman in charge was Henry Tomkinson. They made most of the decisions while Lionel McArthur stayed in his big house, safe from weather—no matter what that weather might be.

It wasn't living on the McArthur ranch that had Donald feeling melancholy. It was because he wanted more. He'd been wanting more for a very long time. He had just turned twenty-nine and was feeling his age. What would happen when he turned thirty? Would women even want him anymore?

He ran one hand through thick, wavy brown hair, lifting his eyes from his work and looking through the window in front of him. He saw Henry pass by and rose quickly to his feet.

He threw open the door of the bunkhouse and poked his head out. Henry was heading for the chow house some twenty yards away.

"Henry," he called out. "Hey."

Henry spun around with an alerted look on his face. He relaxed when he saw who it was.

"Oh, it's you. You gave me a fright."

Donald laughed. "You must be pulling my leg. I said your name first. What killer of men is going to say someone's name first?"

Henry shrugged, coming back toward Donald. "I don't know. You tell me."

"No one, that's who," Donald replied mischievously. "No one is going to call to their victim before they kill them."

"You want to bet me on that?" Henry asked. "What are you doing out here anyway? Ain't you supposed to be out there on the property doing something? Some actual work?"

"The men have it covered. I needed to come in here and fix this saddlebag. I won't be missed."

Henry sighed, a reluctant look on his face. "Well, you ain't lying."

"I reckon that's why you're here, too, right?" Donald teased. "You ain't got nothing better to do?"

"I do have better things to do," Henry said, sounding like those things weren't as important as he was claiming, "Men gotta take breaks sometimes, too."

"And that's why you see me right here," Donald joked.

"Yeah, pining away for a woman, aren't you?"

Donald would have been insulted by the man's teasing if it weren't so much the truth. He'd only entrusted Henry with his dark secret—the fact that he was desperate to marry. He wanted a wife, children—a family—more than anything else in the world. He had to do it before it was too late. He wanted to be young enough to play with his children.

"Hard to believe, ain't it?" he said sarcastically. "I mean, look at me."

Henry reacted, tilting his head to the side, and raising one eyebrow. "Hey, I know you joke, but you aren't a bad-looking fella. Lots of girls would be proud to be on your arm."

Donald grinned. "That's your honest opinion, is it?"

"Yeah," Henry replied, nodding. "It is."

That was one of the things Donald liked the most about Henry. He told the truth. He was blunt but tactful. In ten years of working with the older man, Donald had learned a lot of wisdom. Henry was almost like a father or an uncle to him.

"Well, thanks for that. I'm flattered."

"So you talked to Susie or Sandy lately?"

Susie and Sandy were Donald's sisters. They were twins. The girls had moved to Oklahoma when their parents died, leaving Donald to fend for himself.

"I have to write to them today. They've sent me a couple of letters, and if I don't write them soon, they will show up here to make sure I'm okay."

"What's wrong with that? A little sisterly affection never hurt anybody. Besides," Henry grinned, "I'm pretty sure the men would like to see them, too."

Donald just pursed his lips. His sisters were very good-looking. Unfortunately, he didn't have super high opinions of either of them. Susie had the personality of a grapefruit, and Sandy could barely string two sentences together without praising herself for something or another and seeking praise from others.

He kept his mouth shut, though. They were his sisters, and of course, he loved them even though they were quite unlovable. At times.

"I can do without that much affection. And I don't call it that anyway. I call it control. That's all they want to do. Control me."

Henry just laughed at him. Donald wasn't upset by it. He had complained about his well-meaning sisters for years, but everyone knew he actually loved them both.

"You should write to them then. Let them know you're doing good. Tell them you'll be foreman someday, and they can come and stay in the big house with McArthur."

Donald pulled his eyebrows together. "Now, why would I want to go and tell them something like that? I don't like to lie to my sisters."

"You won't be lying," Henry objected. "You very well could be foreman someday. I'm not going to live forever, am I? And just because I'm the foreman here doesn't mean I'm the old man's favorite. That, my friend, would be *you*." When he said the last word, he reached out and poked Donald in the chest above his heart.

Donald was aware that Lionel McArthur treated him differently from the others. And he also knew why. There was a painting of a man hanging above one of the fireplaces. That man resembled Donald in a remarkable way. When he asked about it, Donald was told that it was not a young Lionel McArthur like he suspected. It was Lionel's father. Apparently, the man was a strong spirit, a gentleman to his core, a fine, loving, upstanding citizen, husband, father. And Lionel had worshipped the ground his Papa had walked on.

The resemblance was so strong, Lionel had mentioned it the first day they met. Donald was instantly hired because of the similarity.

"He does act like I'm related to him, doesn't he?" He didn't form it as a question. It was more of a statement.

Henry nodded, pulling a flask from his back pocket. He unscrewed it and took a long swallow. When he lowered it a couple seconds later, he smacked his lips and let out a sharp breath. "Ahh, nothing like tequila on a hot sunny day." He offered the flask to Donald, who shook his head.

"Too hot for the drink," he said. "At least for me. You go right ahead. It's a free country."

Henry put the lid back on the flask and screwed it tight. He shoved it in his back pocket. "Your loss, fella. I'll tell you what, since it's so hot you don't want to go work the field, why don't you do us all a favor and write to your sisters. You were right. There ain't a reason for them to be here. At all. Write to them. Keep them from coming."

He leaned forward, his voice dropping as if someone might hear him.

"It would be a pretty bad blow to the morale of the crew if your sisters are hanging about pampering you and coddling you like they always do when they are here. You know how annoying they can be."

Donald didn't need any more reminders. "I know, Henry. I know. I'll go in and write to them right now."

"When you're done, go on out to the west side and check that fence about halfway up. Make sure it's not fallen down or looks like it's going to. Somebody told me they saw some cracks in the railings. We can't have that. That bull gets out, and we're done for. He's likely to kill somebody."

Donald nodded, his face turning serious. The bull had gotten out three times in as many months.

He was a dangerous animal, more vicious than the previous bulls kept at the McArthur ranch. Donald fully expected the creature to hurt someone someday.

"I'll get right on that."

"Just make sure that bull stays where he belongs," Henry cautioned.

"I will."

4

———

Aileen sealed the envelope, thinking how it represented her hopes and dreams. She had found an acceptable ad from a man in a town only thirty miles away. He owned a large ranch and was looking for a bride to help him run the estate. He hadn't mentioned children, which Aileen saw as an opportunity to have some of her own. He sounded pleasant enough from the short ad, and she was anxious to find out more about him.

The sun would be setting in a few hours. At that moment, it was shining directly on the flower garden, a place where she and Theresa had spent many days walking, talking, sitting on the benches. There was a large fountain in the middle of the garden, a sculpture of roses with water spurting from within the petals. It was such beautiful land-scaping, Aileen couldn't help wondering if the ranch in Gustaf's Corner was just as beautiful. The one she would be going to, hopefully. She wished she didn't have to wait to hear back from the man, even though she knew absolutely nothing about him at that point. Nothing other than his name.

Lionel McArthur.

It was a nice-sounding name. Very classy, she felt. She knew enough about living the wealthy life, even though she herself had never been wealthy. She was willing to learn.

The thought made Aileen giggle. She saw someone emerge from below her vision and took several steps toward the window to see who it was.

Theresa. She was walking alone through the garden. She didn't have any of the children with her.

Sadness swept over Aileen. She reached out and placed her fingertips on the glass as if she was touching Theresa from afar. Her best friend. The woman who had saved her from a life of poverty and sadness. Theresa was like her sister.

Aileen tucked the letter into her apron pocket and hurried to her door. She rushed down the stairs and out the door, hoping Theresa was still in the garden and wouldn't mind some company.

Theresa was, in fact, still in the garden and had taken a seat on one of the benches she and Theresa often occupied together. She made her way down the path quickly, being careful where she put her feet so she didn't step in the slightly muddy dirt from the rain earlier that afternoon. The sun couldn't reach the area under the flowerbeds, so they remained wet and would be all night.

"Theresa," she said as she approached, keeping her voice soft. If she unintentionally scared the woman, she didn't want to do it by barking her name.

Theresa looked swiftly over at her and smiled. Aileen was sure she saw sadness in that smile, and it didn't reach Theresa's eyes.

"Hello, dear. What are you doing? Taking a walk?"

Aileen nodded. "I was thinking about it, yes. Might go into town before it gets too dark. Would you like to come?"

She sat down next to Theresa and studied her friend's face. There was something off about the way Theresa was looking at her. She couldn't help feeling self-conscious, as if she'd done something wrong. But there was only one thing she had been doing lately that might upset Theresa. And she was fairly certain her friend didn't know about her mail order bride business.

"I don't think so, Aileen," Theresa answered her, shaking her head lightly. "I know you have things to do in town, and I don't want to interfere."

Aileen tilted her head to the side, giving Theresa an inquisitive look. "Whatever are you talking about, Theresa? I love having you with me when I go to town."

Theresa hesitated before she said, "Do you?"

Aileen blinked at her friend. "What's going on, Theresa? Please tell me what you're thinking. Something has upset you."

"You know what's upset me," Theresa responded in a curt voice.

Aileen's heart pounded. She frowned. "Theresa. Tell me what you're talking about."

Theresa looked away from her, staring at the fountain like she'd never seen it before. "I saw the magazine. I know you're leaving us. I just wish I understood why. Are you lonely? Do we not treat you like family? Why would you want to go away?"

Aileen hadn't been expecting this conversation. She pressed her lips together and tried to think quickly. What words would best explain how she was feeling?

"Theresa, you have been the best friend I could ever have. The opportunities I've had with you are so wonderful. And I do want my thirtieth birthday party to be here with all of you. But I have to find a life of my own now."

Theresa didn't look comforted. Aileen could see she was wrestling with herself.

"I don't want you to be unhappy," Theresa responded in a tight voice. "I don't want you to go either. Isn't there anyone here in Shady Forks you can fall in love with?"

Aileen had to laugh softly. "No. I'm afraid not."

"But what if someone moves here after you're gone, and they would have been perfect for you?"

Aileen stared at Theresa for a moment. "What if that doesn't happen for seven years and the man I find through the magazine falls in love with me and treats me wonderfully? I need encouragement during this transition, Theresa. I need you to understand why I want to find a life of my own. Just like you did."

"But you came with me," Theresa complained, sounding like a little girl. Aileen couldn't be angry with her. She was acting like the teenager she'd been when they met. "And I didn't think you were going to stay for a little while and then leave. You're supposed to be *my* companion. You're supposed to be with *me*."

Aileen shook her head. "You don't belong to me, and I don't belong to you. That's you and Nate. It's his job to be with you and be a best friend and companion. Not mine. Not anymore. Not that I don't want to be or that I don't love you. I do. But I have to find my way in this world, and soon I will be too old to do that. I'm hoping to someday have children of my own. Don't you want that for me?"

Theresa sighed. "Of course I do. I really do. I want you to be happy like I am."

"Then you've got to support me on this. And if things work out the way I'm hoping, I won't really be that far away."

Theresa's eyebrows shot up. "You've found someone already?"

"Yes. Gustaf's Corner. A wealthy rancher there is looking for a woman to come and help him run his estate."

"Well, that's certainly something you can do. You've been working with Aggie this whole time, making sure the household is running smoothly. Mostly with the children, of course, but you've been just a dream for us all this whole time. What will we do without you?"

Aileen gazed at her friend affectionately. "I'm sure you will get along just fine. I'm kind of a fifth wheel here in this house, don't you think? It's time for me to find a husband of my own and have a family."

"Yes." Theresa sounded more determined than anything now. She turned to Aileen and grabbed her by the shoulders. "We'll have a birthday party and a going-away party mixed into one. It will be grand. We'll tell everyone your good news and—"

Aileen laughed. "Wait, Theresa, hold your horses. I am just now writing to this man. Let's wait and see if he decides I'm the one he chooses. I'm sure he'll get plenty of letters. He sounded very charming in the ad."

"Those ads are so short," Theresa mentioned. "You can't really tell much from them. But we'll be keeping in touch with you, and if the man you go there for isn't a good man, treating you with respect and love, then you just let us know, and we'll come and snatch you back up."

Aileen sighed softly. "You're such a good friend, Theresa. I love you."

Theresa laughed, pulling Aileen into a hug. "I love you, too. I'm so glad you came out to talk to me."

5

The sound of several hammers, all hitting the nails in different patterns, filled the air around Donald. He had just stepped back from his side of the shed, staring at the part of the outer wall he was reinforcing. He lifted his arm and swiped the back of his wrist across his forehead, knocking his hat back a little and letting the sun shine directly in his eyes.

He squinted and yanked his hat back down to block the sun again.

"Donald."

He heard his name being called in the distance.

"Hey, Donald."

He turned away from the barn and had to walk a few steps to look around the line of trees around the shed. He'd recognized Henry's voice but wasn't going to respond until he was looking at the man. He lifted one hand and waved his hammer in the air.

"Over here," he called out.

"Boss wants to see you in his office," Henry yelled, not coming any closer.

Donald nodded and waved his hammer again. "Yep. All right. Let me pack up and wash up."

"He said soon as you can." Henry's voice carried across the field.

Donald nodded again.

Henry turned and walked away, heading back to do whatever work he was already doing when he got Donald's message.

Donald pulled his work gloves off, glancing at the shed, where two of the other ranch hands had been working with him to reinforce the walls. The recent rains had revealed several spots that were leaking through the exterior walls and the roof. The roof would be done next, after the walls.

He pulled the handkerchief from his back pocket and swiped it across his forehead as he made his way to his horse. He untied the animal from the low-hanging branch the reins were thrown over and got up in the saddle.

"Let's go see what the old man wants," he said.

He thought about Lionel McArthur as he rode to the huge house where the little man lived. To Donald, it was like burying one pharaoh in one pyramid in Egypt. Thousands of square feet, reaching up into the heavens. For one man.

Nevertheless, Donald had plenty of affection for the man. There was no doubt he favored Donald because of the likeness to his own father. They weren't related, though. Donald was sure of that.

He tried to never take advantage of the old man's kind heart. He was determined to give the respect he was given.

He left his horse in front of the house and skipped every other step as he went up to the porch. He'd been in the house many times and knew exactly where Lionel's office was.

One of the best things about working for Lionel McArthur was the man's generous and friendly nature. It was a boost to the morale of the inside and outside staff that their employer truly seemed to care about their welfare and happiness. He paid good wages and treated everyone with respect.

He got to the man's door, but before he knocked, he straightened his vest, used his handkerchief once more to wipe his face, and took a few seconds to wish he'd stopped at the bunkhouse to wash up a bit. He could only hope he didn't stink.

He knocked and opened the door when he heard Lionel's voice.

"Donald. Come in."

He was greeted with enthusiasm and walked into the stylish office, where his boss was seated behind his large mahogany desk with unique carvings along all the edges.

Lionel McArthur stood up, but he might as well have continued sitting. He had shrunk over the years and hadn't been that tall to begin with. He was also exceedingly skinny so that the skin that had once been young and perfect hung at his jowls and under his eyes ever so slightly.

Despite his advanced years, Lionel had sparkling blue eyes that darted about inquisitively, probably the only thing left on his body that moved quickly. His brain was still as sharp as a tack, too. Donald wouldn't have wanted to go up against him in a battle of wits.

"It's good to see you, boss. How are you feeling these days?"

"Oh, it's coming to the end, my friend. But I'm still alive and kicking for now. I've got plans, and I'm not going anywhere until I see them through."

"That's the spirit, sir." Donald clenched one fist in the air in front of him, making the old man grin wide.

Lionel waved his hand at the chair opposite him on the other side of his desk.

"Please, sit. I want to speak to you for a moment if you have time."

"I always have time for you, Mr. McArthur," Donald said respectfully. He sat in the chair he was directed to and placed his hat on his knee. He was glad to take it off and to get out of the sun. It was cooler in the house than it was outside, and a nice breeze was blowing in through the windows, filled with the scent of upcoming rain.

"That's nice of you to say," the man responded. "Now I've got a proposal for you, Donald, and I hope that you will accept this opportunity. I need someone to go to the stagecoach station in one hour to pick up a young lady."

He stopped, and Donald could only guess that was to give him time to process what he'd just been told. "I'm at your disposal. Is that all you need me to do? Where will I be taking her?"

Lionel sat forward. "I need to tell you a story first. Do you have a little time?"

Donald shrugged. "I work for you," he stated bluntly.

Lionel nodded. "You've been here for ten years, is that right?"

"It's coming up on that, yes."

Lionel sat back. His sharp eyes wandered around the room as he spoke, and he laced his fingers together over his flat stomach. "I started out as a man with a small fortune, Donald, and when I say small fortune, I mean only a few hundred dollars. I built up my estate here and my business and my wealth using my own wit and ingenuity. I have always considered myself to be exceedingly smart." He tapped his forehead with one thin index finger. "I've got a lot going on up here. Even now. But unfortunately, I never let my heart be taken by a woman. I was fifty years old before I got married, and I did that because I saw myself dying without loving anyone or being loved and leaving all of this to charity." He swept his hand around.

"Yes, sir," Donald said to show he was listening.

"Well, now I find myself, thirty years later, a widower with two of the nastiest, low-life stepsons I could ever have imagined having. Those two will stop at nothing to get my money. I don't want them to have it." He slammed his fist down on the desktop, making Donald jump in surprise. He hadn't expected such a move from the small man. "I *won't* let them have it. I have sent for a woman to come to Gustaf's Corner and be my bride. She will be the one to inherit everything I have."

Donald sat in shock, not believing what he was hearing.

"I want you to pick her up and go to the justice of the peace who will be waiting for you. The arrangements have been made. You will stand in for me and marry her to make her my wife. She will inherit all of this."

Donald's eyebrows shot up. "I am to marry her? Is that legal, sir?"

"I will be marrying her," Lionel stated firmly. "And you will stand in for me, as I am unable to leave the house. Please don't ask any questions and just do as you are told. I trust you, Donald. More than anyone else on this ranch, I trust you. Will you help me with this?"

Donald blinked rapidly, a thousand thoughts running through his head. "Uh, okay," he said.

Why not help the man out? It might turn into an interesting adventure.

6

onald left the house still trying to process everything his boss had told him.

The woman's name was Aileen Riley. She'd been chosen out of five ladies who had answered the old man's bridal ad in the magazine. He was to pick her up and take her to marry her—that is, to stand in for Lionel and bring her back to the estate that would someday be completely hers.

He couldn't believe it.

Lionel hadn't told him whether or not the woman knew what she was getting into. Donald didn't know how to feel about that. He went in search of Henry to talk to him about it.

He found the foreman behind the stable, chucking hay over a fence line.

"Henry," he said, getting the older man's attention. Henry was nearing fifty and had worked the McArthur ranch for twice as long as Donald. He had a family, and he and his wife lived in a cottage on the McArthur land, several acres from the main house.

"Donald, what'd he want?"

"He's sending me to town. I'm to pick up a lady."

Henry narrowed his eyes, ceasing his hay baling and stabbing the pitchfork down into the ground, holding onto the handle.

"What?"

Donald lifted his eyebrows. "You heard me. Gotta pick up a lady and take her to the justice of the peace. Marry her as a stand-in for Lionel."

The astonished look on Henry's face reflected how Donald was feeling. "You're pulling my leg," Henry finally said.

Donald shook his head. "No, sir. I gotta go marry a fine lady this afternoon and bring her back here."

"Well, is she almost a hundred like McArthur?'

Donald laughed. "No. He said she's a young lady. I don't know how old she is, but I'm willing to bet she's under forty. That would be young to him, wouldn't it?"

"Sixty is young to Lionel McArthur," Henry joked.

It was all in fun. Donald knew someone would be hard-pressed to find anyone on the ranch that didn't have some affection for the old man.

"Well, I'm about to head out there and pick her up. Her name is Aileen."

"What's she look like?"

"He didn't say. I don't imagine there's a whole lot of people taking a stagecoach to Gustaf's Corner, though. She'll probably be alone."

"You're right. Hadn't thought of that." He let his last words drift in the air, looking away from Donald. "A woman coming here. As mistress of the house." He shook his head, taking off his hat and rubbing his sweaty forehead. "That's gonna be a real change. I guess I should go and warn everybody."

"I wonder why he didn't tell you about this," Donald said. "You're the head foreman. You should know about changes like that."

"I'm sure he told Bertie and the other ladies working in the house," Henry replied in a reasonable voice. "They're the ones that will have to deal with her. I won't."

"Wrong," Donald said gently. He maintained steady eye contact with the foreman. "McArthur is only having this lady come here because he thinks he's going to die soon, and he doesn't want Conrad and Buster to get his estate or any of his money."

Henry reacted to the name of Lionel's two step-sons by curling his lip and spitting on the ground near him. "Ugh. Don't even say their names," he grumbled. "God knows he's doing the right thing by that."

"I can't believe he doesn't have any friends or any other family he's willing to leave it to."

"Well, you gotta also remember that anyone he leaves it to is gonna have a fight on their hands. Them boys aren't gonna let anyone have this place *and* all the money. They'll think they're entitled to it—probably all of it—just because their mother was married to Lionel."

"They don't deserve a penny of it," Donald said, nodding. "That's true. And I guess he doesn't want any of his friends to have to go through all that harassment from those two after he's gone."

Henry sighed through his nose. "You think he's really gonna die soon?" he asked in a voice that made him sound younger than Donald.

Donald shrugged.

"I don't know," he responded. "I hope not. I wish

he could live on another twenty years. God knows he's got the spirit for it."

"He does, doesn't he?" Henry laughed.

"Ironic that you want to get married so much, and here you're gonna get some practice, eh?"

Donald shared a laugh with his friend. "Yeah. I get practice. That's where it will end, though. She's not gonna be married to me. I asked the boss if that was legal, and he seemed to think it was. I guess since he signed the papers and all, I'm just a body."

Henry threw back his head and let out a sharp laugh. "If that's what it takes to get in a little practice, I say, go for it. Does she know he's sending you?"

Donald shrugged. "I don't think so. I'm not gonna be the one to explain it either. That's gonna be his job."

"Well, I hope it all works out. The old man is brilliant and usually makes some pretty good plans. He's got a brain in there, just as sharp as he was twenty, thirty, forty years ago."

"Yeah, I hope I'm like that when I'm old like him."

"Well, you aren't now. So go on and get married. I'll see you back here in a couple of hours. You come and tell me everything that happens. You got that?"

Donald nodded. "I will."

He turned and walked away as Henry grabbed his pitchfork out of the ground and jabbed it into the haystack in front of him.

As Donald walked to the stable, he studied the land around him, thinking about how long he'd been there. He was so used to it, he barely noticed his surroundings anymore. He had a feeling any young lady coming to the ranch and seeing its beauty wouldn't be able to resist wanting it for themselves. She wouldn't have to be greedy to want it. And to have it presented on a silver platter... what could be better than that?

He had a little time to contemplate how he would go about the next few hours while he got the buggy ready, hitched up the horses, and drove to the station. He wasn't at all nervous, which surprised him. It was something Lionel had arranged, and he trusted his boss.

The only question on his mind was whether or not he should try to explain the situation to the woman. He didn't want Lionel's plans to fall through. He understood that the old man didn't want Aileen to know anything until she actually got there and was already married to Lionel McArthur.

She would see the ranch first. Before she saw the old man. That might make a difference, especially when he told her he would be giving it all to her if she stayed married to him.

It would take quite a woman to agree to that. She might feel cheated. Not Donald nor anyone else on the ranch would let this Aileen woman disrespect or hurt Lionel in any way. They would make sure if she wasn't willing to treat him with the loving kindness he deserved, she would be out on her rear. They would find a replacement for her.

Donald felt it was his responsibility to protect Lionel and that was exactly what he planned to do.

7

Aileen was peering intently out the stagecoach window as they pulled into the station, looking for the man who had sent for her. She was surprised to see there was only one man there, and he was young and dapper, looking a bit rugged for a man of great wealth.

He had to be there to pick her up. There were no other passengers on the stagecoach. She had ridden the entire way by herself, peacefully reading to pass the time.

Now, her heart was beating double-time, and her skin tingled with excitement, especially after seeing the handsome Lionel McArthur.

She stepped out of the coach, taking the hand of

the good-looking man. He was smiling so wide, looking so charming. She was delighted she'd made the decision to come to Gustaf's Corner.

"Aileen Riley?" he asked, his voice deep and smooth.

She nodded. "Yes, that's me."

"I'm so glad to see you. I hope you had a good trip?"

"It was a bit boring," Aileen admitted, feeling comfortable with the man already. He seemed more like a ranch hand than a businessman to her. That felt like a win-win to her. "So I'm glad I'm here."

"Do you want to get something to eat before we go to the justice of the peace for the marriage ceremony?"

Aileen blinked at him. When she had gone with Theresa to Shady Forks, Nate had offered her rooms in their ranch, but she and Theresa had stayed in the boarding house for quite a while before Theresa felt comfortable going through with the ceremony. This felt very rushed to her.

The stagecoach driver brought her two large trunks over and set them down next to Lionel. "Here you go," he said, holding out one hand. The man gave him two coins, which made the driver smile wide. "Thank you, sir."

Lionel turned back to her. "So, do you want some food or off to the justice of peace ?"

Aileen thought quickly. She had come for adventure and change. This was a little fast, but not everyone was going to be patient like Nate Winchester. This man wanted to get married right away. And why shouldn't she? He was very good-looking. He seemed intelligent and looked like he knew what a hard day's work was, which was more than Aileen could say for many of the wealthy men in Boston.

"I suppose we can just go to the justice of the peace now. I brought along sandwiches, and we stopped in Hollow Junction so I could get something there."

"Sounds good. That's an interesting accent. Where are you from originally?"

"Boston," Aileen replied with a grin. It was something she hadn't mentioned in her letters. It was nice to know she still had something of an accent left, considering she'd moved to the west years ago.

"Ah. I've never been out of Wyoming."

He was quiet as he led her to the buggy, carrying the luggage like they weighed no more than a feather. She happened to know they were both quite heavy, stuffed with everything she owned. The

Winchesters had tried to get her to take more, but she'd made them promise to keep anything else she had left behind safe, and she would return for it someday. Or not. They could use whatever they found of hers.

Thinking about Theresa and her family made Aileen's heart ache. She was missing them already.

"I don't know if you noticed, but I only came from thirty miles away, in Shady Forks."

Lionel lifted his eyebrows. "Is that so? I think I may have been there once or twice. Just passing through or stopping for an auction, though. I don't recognize you."

"Do you know the Winchesters?" she asked anxiously. She was only a little disappointed when he shook his head. The family had told her they didn't recognize the name Lionel McArthur either. "That's okay. I was staying with them in Shady Forks. That's been my home for four years. Before that, I was in the employment of the Baldwin family as a companion for their only daughter, Theresa."

"And was that something you enjoyed?" he asked.

Aileen nodded. "Oh yes. The whole family are very nice people. Theresa was a little bit outgoing, I guess you could say. Headstrong."

"Stubborn," Lionel supplied.

Aileen nodded. "Yes, exactly. And she decided she wanted to leave Boston. There were no men there that interested her."

"That's got to be a lot of men to choose from, though, isn't it?"

She thought about it and had to agree with him. "Yes. But Theresa was a unique girl. She really knew what she wanted all the time, and that's what she'd go for. She's a very good friend to me."

"I'm sure you miss her, don't you?" The sympathy in his voice made Aileen's heart melt.

She nodded. "Yes. I do. I just left them, and I feel like half my heart is gone."

"I'm sure you'll make plenty of good friends at the ranch," he stated confidently. "You seem like a very nice lady. Everyone will love you, I'm sure."

Aileen grinned wide. She had been hearing that quite a lot lately. To hear it from a stranger she'd only exchanged a few letters with made it all the more profound in her mind.

The man in the community center justice of the peace office opened his own door and shook Lionel's hand as they came in. He held out his arm to them, allowing them to pass in front of him. He closed the door and turned to them, crossing the room rubbing his hands together as if he was ready to start an experiment.

"How are you both today?" he asked.

"Doing well, thank you," Aileen responded.

Lionel just nodded.

"I'm just going to go through the simple words here, and you just respond with I do, all right?"

Aileen was surprised by the informal setting and the casual nature of the ceremony. She remembered Theresa's grand wedding and felt a little hurt that she hadn't merited that same kind of reception from the man who had sent for her.

Glancing at him, Aileen couldn't help thinking he looked incredibly nervous. When the justice of the peace asked him if he would take her to be his bride, he said, "Uh, yeah." The man behind the desk had to tell him to say, "I do."

Despite the strangeness of it all, Aileen went through with it. She promised herself that she would get her grand wedding after she and Lionel had bonded some more. She would win him over, and he would want to give her the best wedding of all time.

Feeling more positive, Aileen left the community center feeling like Mrs. Lionel McArthur, even though she got absolutely no fanfare and there was no one there to congratulate her.

She climbed back into the buggy to go to her new home, wishing she'd asked Theresa to at least come with her and keep her company for a week or two. That's what she'd done for Theresa, except she never left. Theresa would return home.

She tried not to feel weepy as they rode down the rocky road, heading out of town. She swallowed her tears and forced herself to think only good things. Theresa would be happy for her to see what a handsome man she'd married. Maybe the house was as beautiful as the man was.

"Why don't you tell me a little about yourself," Lionel said after they had been quiet for a good ten minutes and the town was just being left behind.

"I don't know what to tell you that I didn't put in my letters," Aileen said quietly. "I'll be very honest with you, I don't remember all that I wrote. I was excited about being chosen and was, I must say, anxious to come to Gustaf's Corner and start anew."

"You became unhappy in Shady Forks? You are still friends with Theresa and her family, aren't you?"

Aileen nodded emphatically. "Oh yes," she said. "It was just time. I wasn't exactly unhappy. It was just time for me to get my own life, you know? And I'm hoping that's what I've got now, here in your hometown."

He gave her a wavering smile that she didn't understand. "I hope you're happy here, Aileen. I really do."

8

Donald was taken aback by the beauty of the woman who stepped off the stage-coach. It was the first thing he'd noticed. In his experience, women who looked like that were usually unpleasant and filled with self-importance.

He could tell from the moment she opened her mouth and smiled at him, she wasn't one of those women. She probably did have the Irish hot temper that her red hair signified, but she was far from unpleasant. Her green eyes sparkled at him.

He hadn't known how to act in the justice of the peace office. He'd gone ahead with the ceremony, trying not to show how incredibly nervous he'd been. The justice of the peace must have been in on the deception because he never once questioned why a man fifty years younger than Lionel McArthur was standing in his place.

Lionel had said all the arrangements were already made.

Aileen obviously didn't know what was going on. His loyalty to his boss didn't waver, and he never considered telling Aileen the truth once he'd made up his mind not to.

It wasn't until they were on their way to the ranch, after the ceremony, that Donald realized he might have just made a very bad mistake. Once Aileen found out he had played a part in deceiving her, catching her in a trap, she was going to hate him. She would treat him terribly, especially after Lionel died and could no longer protect him.

He glanced at her profile as she chatted away about her friend Theresa Winchester and the rest of her friend's family back in Shady Forks. Was she the vindictive type? Would she take it out on him, the deception that Lionel had perpetrated on her?

He swallowed hard, turning his eyes back to the road in front of him. He didn't want that. She did seem like such a nice lady. He'd made sure to treat her with respect from the moment he picked her up. Maybe being nice to her would ease the pain when she found out what he'd done. What he'd helped Lionel do. She was bound by a contract she had signed. She was married to Lionel, whether she liked it or not.

If that was practice for what it would really be like to marry, Donald didn't feel it. The only thrill he'd had from getting married that afternoon was the thrill of fear for when Aileen would find out what had been done to her. She'd been Shanghaied. And he'd been a part of it. A big part.

His stomach hurt. How was she going to react to all this?

He made a vow to himself that he would drop her off at Lionel's office and get out of there quick. He'd go find Henry and hide out for a while. No telling what this redhead would do when she was angry. Or *how* angry all this would make her. He didn't know her well enough to predict what her reaction would be.

"Is this your family's property that we're going to?" she asked curiously. "Were you born and raised at the McArthur ranch?"

Donald's thoughts raced as he tried to decide how to handle the questions. "I... I wasn't born and raised there. I've been living there for some time now, though. I really think you will like it. Everyone does. All the crew and the household staff say it's one of the best places to work."

Aileen raised her eyebrows, giving him an impressed look. He clenched his jaw. If he continued talking, he would reveal what station he really had at the ranch, just by the way he spoke of his coworkers. He doubted Lionel spoke of his employees that way.

He thought for a moment about expanding on the lie, embellishing so he could speak, but he shied away from the idea, realizing it would only make things worse when she found out who he really was.

"So, how many people do you have working for you?"

He hesitated. "There are six men on the grounds, two of them mostly for landscaping, you know, the garden and flowerbeds and the like. Foreman and second foreman. Inside the house is..." He had to let his words trail off. He had no idea how many people were employed inside the house. He tried to think quickly. Were there two maids? Three? One? He knew there was a housekeeper and a groom out in the stables. He chuckled and smiled at her. "I'm really not sure how many employees are in the house. That's left up to Bertie. The housekeeper."

"Ah." Aileen nodded, a satisfied look on her face.

Relief swept through him. he was able to get through that without blundering too much.

"You have a cook?"

Donald nodded immediately. "Yes. Cook. Irene. She's a wonder. Really good food. She lets the ranch hands have leftovers, and there's usually a lot of those. Mister... There's always too much for one person to eat."

"You don't have guests a lot?"

Donald tilted his head and thought about it. He hadn't seen a lot of people visiting Mr. McArthur. There were some regulars—his lawyer, his personal doctor, and of course Anne Ross, his secretary. But as for social calls, he didn't really think Mr. McArthur had a lot of friends.

"Not too many social calls, I'm afraid," he said.

"So not a lot of parties for me to host then?"

She sounded relieved. He decided she was and went with that. "No. You don't have to worry about that. If you ever want to have a party, I'm sure it will be perfectly fine. You just have to let everyone know. The staff, I mean." He hoped he wasn't blushing. It was getting increasingly harder not to reveal who he was.

"You're pretty sure it will be fine?" She grinned at him. "Don't you make that decision?"

He tried to smile back and let out a short, raspy laugh. "What I mean is, to make sure there are no conflicts in schedules, you see. Everyone will be on board and know what needs to be done when it needs to be done. Efficiency is the key, you know. That's one of the keys, anyway, to making money. Making sure things run efficiently."

He glanced at her to see if he'd impressed her with his short speech. It looked like he'd succeeded by the soft smile she was giving him, a look that was reflected in her eyes. It was something he'd heard Lionel say years before and had never forgotten. Then again, Henry hadn't forgotten either and frequently espoused efficiency, noting that Lionel had pushed for it, which made it important to them all.

As they got closer to the ranch, Donald realized he was approaching doom. He'd known a few redheads in his life. They'd had some pretty nasty tempers on them. He was definitely only leaving her at Lionel's office and skedaddling out of there.

It was too bad that he hadn't really married the woman, though. By the time they got to the ranch and pulled onto the property, he had decided she was funny, sweet, mild-tempered, and beautiful beyond words. He had a feeling his initial thoughts on her beauty would prove to be both inside and out.

When Aileen gasped, Donald glanced at her. Her eyes had widened, and she was looking all around them. The dirt road up to the ranch was fairly long, flanked by extremely tall pines. They made a wall between the road and the rest of the land, but the vast front lawn could be seen through the spaces in between. She was moving her head back and forth, looking around the pines, taking in whatever she could see on the other side. Her jaw was slack. He could see she was highly impressed.

He didn't know why he was filled with satisfaction. This land wasn't his.

"This is absolutely beautiful," she whispered breathlessly. "Oh my, you have such good taste. Spare no expense, I see. My goodness. My goodness." She laughed abruptly, and he turned to see she was watching two of the dogs playing in the field.

He wished he could take credit for it all. But none of it was his.

9

"It is beautiful," Lionel said in a plain voice.

Aileen glanced at him, amazed that he would be so humble about his beautiful home. She looked up at the tops of the pines as they passed, down to their trunks where grass and flowers grew. The dogs playing in the distance, obviously not fighting, as there was no growling but a lot of jumping in the air.

She spotted several horses in the distance, men in the saddles on their backs, moving through a herd of plump, healthy-looking cattle.

The house came better into view as they went around a slight curve. She'd been able to see the top of it when they pulled onto the dirt road. That was another thing she noticed immediately. As soon as they turned off the main road out of town, the ground became smooth. The path to the house was raked and gutted of rocks and twigs, tree branches, and anything else that might cause the horses to stumble or the buggy to rock.

The house rose upward into the sky like a castle. The windows were narrow at the top, coming up to a peak, while the bottoms were flat. They dotted the rounded walls, revealing nothing on the inside but blackness. The sun was shining directly on the front of the house, bringing out how white it was. The windows had yellow shutters on either side, open to let the sunshine in.

"You are very humble, you know that?" she said, smiling at him. "This house is absolutely stunning."

She didn't quite understand the look he gave her. He almost looked afraid. But why would he be afraid of her? She wasn't going to harm him.

They pulled up in front of the house and were greeted by three dogs. "Hello, boys," Lionel said, getting down from the buggy and going around to help her down. "I'll get the bags and bring them up to the porch. One of the ladies will take them to your room, I'm sure."

His words were a relief to Aileen's ears. That meant he at least was not prepared to force her to do anything she was uncomfortable doing. Her own room meant a little privacy and time to adjust.

However, she wondered why there were no servants around to help him with the luggage. Why was he doing all the work himself?

She shrugged off her doubts and waited for him so they could walk up the porch steps together.

"Would you like to look around the house before —" He cut himself off abruptly, sending a bit of nervousness through Aileen. Before what? She desperately wanted to know what he was going to say. "What I mean to say is that I can show you around before you get settled in if you'd like."

Aileen nodded. She couldn't help wondering if that was really what he was going to say.

Regardless, he was a good-looking, charming man and she was married to him. She wasn't going to let anything stand in the way of winning his heart. She wanted him to see that she could be adaptive and would quickly adjust to any eccentricities he had. He obviously had some, since he was dressed the way he was and was so standoffish toward her, despite the fact that he was one of the wealthiest men in the area.

He looked nervous when they were approached by a woman in a smart, clean, ironed outfit. She felt sorry for him and stepped up to greet the woman.

"Hello. I'm Aileen Riley. Well, Aileen McArthur now, I suppose." She looked over her shoulder at the man she'd married and grinned wide. "Isn't that right?" She was a little surprised by the hard look the man was giving the young girl. The girl, however, was hiding a giggle behind her hand, moving her eyes from Aileen to Lionel and back.

"I know who you are," she said. She took Aileen's hand and shook it gently before letting go. "I'm Mary. I do the scullery work with Irene. She's the cook. Sometimes I work with Belle. She's in charge of the rooms and such. Dusting and all that. I'm glad you're here, Miss... Mrs. McArthur."

"Oh, that name is long, isn't it?" Aileen said, trying to be gracious the way she'd seen Theresa act toward her servants in Boston. "Just call me Aileen."

Mary blinked at her. Aileen got the distinct impression she hadn't expected that. "All right, ma'am. Thank you. I've got to... get back to work now." She scurried past them, giving a long look to Lionel as she went by him. He returned the look and even turned his head as she went by, still holding eye contact with the girl.

That was a very strange thing to Aileen. It

made her heart beat harder, and her stomach turn. Her husband was a very handsome man, of that there was no doubt. But if she fell in love with him and found him to be an unfaithful cheater, she would be heartbroken. That wasn't love, as far as she was concerned. And love was her ultimate goal.

Lionel turned his eyes back to her. He must have realized he'd been staring at Mary because his face suddenly turned red.

"You should probably catch her and tell her to bring in the luggage, shouldn't you?"

He blinked at her for a moment before reacting with surprise. "Oh. You mean Mary?" He jabbed both thumbs over his shoulder in Mary's direction. She had gone through the front door and was crossing the porch. "Right. Yeah. I should."

Aileen watched as he spun around and hurried to the door, calling out, "Uh, Mary. Mary. Uh, would you mind bringing her bags in and, uh, putting them in the room you probably made up for her?"

"I didn't make the room up," Aileen heard Mary reply even though she couldn't see the girl. "That was Theresa. But I'll bring her bags in and take them up. Don't worry."

"I really appreciate that, Mary," Lionel

responded. Aileen was amazed by the relief and gratitude she saw on his face and heard in his voice.

"Really, don't worry about it, D... sir. Sorry."

Lionel stiffened when the girl apologized. Aileen was fascinated by the strange scene. He turned back around and came over to her, holding out one hand. His face was extremely red.

"I'd like to show you around the bottom floor real quick, so you have your bearings when you are trying to get around. I'm sure you will want to know where the kitchen is when you want a snack and where the library is when you want to read, don't you?"

Aileen felt a tingle of excitement when he mentioned the library.

"You have a library?"

"There are a lot of books in there. I hope there's some you haven't read. I can tell you are probably a reader."

"Why do you say that?"

He grinned. "You just have that look about you. That's a good thing."

She smiled. "It is? Do you like to read?"

"I do," he responded immediately, nodding. Suddenly, his face reddened again, and he cleared his throat. "Let me show you around."

They walked around the bottom floor, Lionel opening up all the doors and letting her look in. When he opened the door to the library, she made to take a step in, but he caught her by the arm.

"I'm afraid we need to make one more stop before you can come back in and take a look at the books. I'm sorry."

It took Aileen by surprise. She blinked at him and stepped back out in the hallway. He led her to a door two down from the library, skipping the one in between. She didn't say anything, curious to know what was going on.

He opened the door and let her go in first, holding his hand out. She was confused and stepped in, looking directly at an elderly man sitting behind a massive desk that looked twice as big as he was.

"Here she is, sir," Lionel said from behind him.

Aileen glanced over her shoulder at him. Fear sliced through her heart when he returned her gaze and slowly closed the door, a look of regret on his handsome face.

10
———

"Please," the old man said, holding out one thin hand toward the chair in front of his desk. "Have a seat. I'd like to talk to you if you don't mind."

Aileen hesitated, staying where she was for a few moments. When he simply smiled at her, she took several steps and dropped into the chair, holding her bag against her chest like it was armor and would prove a worthy shield.

"What... what's going on?" she asked in a tight, frightened voice. Was this Lionel's father? Grandfather? Was he the one who ran the business? Is that why Lionel had been so standoffish?

"I can see you are frightened," the old man said.

"Please don't be. I didn't and don't intend to harm you in any way. In fact, I plan to make you a very, very wealthy woman."

Aileen stared at him, not believing her ears. "Who are you?" she asked breathlessly.

"I am Lionel Arnold McArthur. This is my estate, and I want to leave it in your care when I go on to the next realm."

Aileen stared at him in wonder. Her eyes darted to the door and then back at the elderly man. "You are... then who was it that married me this afternoon?"

Lionel stood up and came around the desk. He was extremely well dressed, in a suit that was obviously made for him, as it fit him wonderfully and made him look as dapper as ever. Aileen was surprised by the flicker of daughterly affection she felt light up in her chest. His eyes were the brightest, sharpest blue Aileen had ever seen on anyone of any age.

His smile was warm. He leaned back against his desk, which dwarfed him. "My dear, I don't want you to be afraid because you will be well taken care of. That man that brought you here and stood in for me at the ceremony is named Donald Ferris. Of all my ranch hands, he is the one I trust the most. He is a good man and will do no harm to anyone. He did what he did as a favor to me, and I do hope you will forgive him for it. He did not ask to be drawn into a deception, which I'm afraid is what has been done to you."

Aileen felt a chill cover her. Lionel's name was Donald. This elderly man was her husband, Lionel McArthur. Anger began to make her feel hot inside. She clenched her jaw.

"Why would you do something like this?" she hissed. "Why would you deceive a young woman into coming here and marrying you? What makes you think this wealth is what I wanted in life? This is not what has been my goal in life."

She felt like standing up and walking out. But there was something about the little man in front of her that made her pause. She wanted to hear his reason. She had asked the question genuinely.

"I have a very good reason for what I've done," Lionel said, giving her a look of compassion. She couldn't help relaxing under his gaze. He crossed his ankles and leaned forward at the waist, looking her directly in the eye. "I need your help, Aileen. I've come to the point that I can only count on you. You and Donald. I hope and pray that I'm not asking too much of you. I know we are strangers now, but I hope that will change in time."

Aileen was still waiting for the good reason. She clutched her bag in her lap so tightly her fingers were going numb. She tried to relax them and found it easier than she'd thought it would be.

"I spent many years pushing people away," Lionel began. "Telling them I didn't need them. I did it to my parents, my siblings, everyone. I wanted to build up this business, and that's all I wanted to do. For fifty years, I worked. Perhaps not as a newborn. I might have taken a few weeks before I got to it."

He smiled at her, and Aileen felt like a warmth emanating from the man. She blinked at him, amazed by the effect he had on her. She wanted to hear more of his story.

"As I said, I pushed everyone away. When I turned fifty, I realized I had to change something. I had no heir. I had no one to take up the business and continue to make it thrive. So I married. I married the lovely Catherine Adelle. She had two small sons. Her husband had been killed in the last war. She was raising those boys on her own, and although I did not fall in love with her right away, I grew to love her. She was a shining star in a dark sky."

Aileen listened to his voice, hearing the love he had for the deceased woman. She tilted her head to the side and refrained from giving him the hug she wanted to give him.

"Sadly, she passed on almost ten years ago. Now I am left with her sons to deal with."

Aileen braced herself. The tone of his voice had suddenly hardened. She immediately didn't like these stepsons he was talking about. She kept her gaze on him, impatient for more of the story.

"Conrad and Buster are two vile creatures," Lionel continued. "They will prey on the weak and vulnerable. They will decimate my property, fire everyone, sell it off and gamble the money away. I cannot let that happen. I've worked all my life for this, and now that I have passed my eightieth birthday, I know I have changed. I have spent the last two or three decades trying to show that I love people and that I should never have pushed anyone away. My siblings and parents have passed on. I am soon to join them, and I feel the urgent need to protect what I have accumulated all these years. I won't let it go to those horrible men." He stopped and leaned toward her again, holding out his hands to her.

Instinctively, she moved to the edge of the seat and rested both her hands in his.

"Will you help me with this, Aileen? Please tell me you will. Nothing will be required of you from me. We will not share a bed. You will have your own suite. You can come and go as you please. You have access to my bank accounts. This is all for you, my dear. All you have to do is promise not to let my stepsons get their hands on my estate. None of it, am I clear? None. No land. No property. No money."

Aileen was taken in by the intensity of his gaze. She almost forgot that he was eighty years old. If she just looked in his eyes, she would swear he was thirty, just like her.

She wanted to be angry. She felt like she might still hold a grudge against Donald for deceiving her the way he did. But she found those feelings had no place where she was at that moment. Lionel needed her. What he'd said made sense to her.

She nodded, a sense of obligation filling her, though there was no reason for her to feel that way. "I'll do what I can, Lionel," she responded firmly. "But they will fight me, won't they? That might be difficult for me. I've never been a confrontational person."

"You will do just fine," Lionel breathed, confidence oozing from his voice. "I know you will do fine. I can see it in those sparkling eyes of yours. Thank you for coming, Aileen. Will you stay?"

Aileen licked her lips and nodded again. "I will stay."

11

Donald went straight from the office to the chow house. It was pulling up on three, which was when the crew usually took a break for coffee or a cold drink and a cigarette if they smoked.

He fully expected at least Henry to be there.

He was relieved when he saw it was only Henry, Buck, and Trevor seated at one of the tables. Buck was one of the hands while Trevor was the crew cook.

"Howdy," the three men greeted him, nearly in unison. They all looked at each other with amused expressions.

"Howdy. You fellas will not believe what I've just been through." He crossed the room and slid into the chair next to Henry, his eyes darting from one to another excitedly. He gestured with his hand, splaying his fingers out. "I am a married man. I just got married."

He chuckled at the expressions on Buck and Trevor's faces. Henry just looked like he was going to laugh. "Yep," he said, nodding. "I knew you were gonna go off and do that."

Donald laughed. "Yeah, because I told you what I was doing this afternoon. She's a real pretty lady, too. I just left her with McArthur. I don't know. I think she might actually stay. She's real reasonable."

"Reasonable?" Trevor and Buck passed a look between them. "What do you mean by reasonable?"

Donald answered Trevor's question. "She'll listen to reason is what I'm saying."

Both men stared at him like he'd lost his mind, and he had to laugh at himself. He hadn't told them anything about what was going on.

"The old man got me to stand in for him to marry this young lady, and he's gonna ask her to stay and take over the property when he dies."

"Oh, you're pulling my leg," Trevor exclaimed. "That's taking a mighty big chance, isn't it? He has no idea what she's like. She's a stranger."

"Would you rather take your chances with a

stranger or have Buster and Conrad come in and destroy this place, fire everyone, and sell it off?" Donald lifted both eyebrows, switching his gaze between the men.

Trevor pursed his lips. "You have a point there," he conceded, nodding. "A trained monkey would be better than Buster and Conrad, those two lying, thieving scoundrels. Not hard to believe they aren't really McArthur's sons. His children would never have grown up like those two. Think they own the world and everyone in it."

Donald listened as the men went on about the boss's decision to bring a strange woman on the property. He tried not to add too much opinion to it, knowing they would catch on to how he was really feeling inside.

For some reason, Donald desperately hoped Lionel could talk Aileen into staying. Her lively chatter on the way home had given him such a good feeling. The McArthur ranch was not known as a negative place to live. In fact, they were never short of staff, and the men worked hard on the land while the women worked hard inside the house. It was a perfect balance. Not to mention they all cared about and respected their boss.

Playing with that delicate balance was dangerous. Bringing a stranger into the mix, whether a man or a woman, was taking a risk with the harmony at the ranch. But it seemed to Donald if there was anyone who could mesh well with how the ranch was run, how well it flowed, it would be Aileen. He'd felt comfortable sitting next to her on the way to the house, even though he was terribly nervous because he was pretending to be someone he wasn't. Even though the thought crossed his mind that she was going to be mad at him, he felt like it wouldn't last.

"So you really think she will stay? Once she realizes what Lionel's done to get her here?" Trevor asked.

Donald lifted the glass of lemonade he'd retrieved for himself while the others were talking. He looked at Trevor over the rim and asked, "I haven't seen her coming asking for a ride back to town, have you?"

Trevor grinned. "Nope. So maybe she is staying. She might make the old man real happy before he dies."

"I doubt they will have an intimate relationship," Henry said in a firm voice. His eyes flicked to Donald. In that instant, Donald knew Henry could tell how he was feeling.

Donald shook his head. "No, that's probably not

in the cards for McArthur anymore. But he's a good man, and he'll treat her right if she stays."

"I'm sure she will become quite loved here," Henry added.

"Well, we aren't gonna torture her, that's for sure," Buck said, lifting a large sandwich to his mouth and taking a bite. "We wouldn't do that to no woman."

Donald looked away as the man spoke while chewing.

Henry tapped him on the arm and gestured toward the door. "Let's get back to work. You ain't done anything since early this afternoon. Just driving a pretty lady around."

Donald chuckled and drank the rest of his lemonade as he stood up. He put the glass back down and nodded at Trevor. "Thanks. I appreciate the cold drink."

"That's what the icebox is for. Anytime, boss."

Henry and Donald left the cook and the ranch hand in the chow house and turned to go in the direction of the shed the men had been working on that day.

"We finished off what we were doing at the shed," Henry said, looking at him. "What you were doing, anyway. And found some more repairs that need to be done before the roof can get started. We don't want to be getting up on that roof just yet, trust me."

Donald nodded. "Whatever you say, boss."

They fell quiet for a minute or so before Henry said, "So this lady. She's real pretty, is she? How old you reckon she is?"

Donald had been waiting for the inquisitive questions. "She is pretty, Henry, wait till you see her. She's got long red wavy hair. It was in a braid, but there were a bunch of strands that got loose, and they were falling down by her cheeks. High cheekbones and these freckles over her nose. The greenest eyes I've ever seen. Probably around my age."

"I knew it," Henry said, stopping in place and turning to him. "You've fallen for her already."

Donald pinched his lips together. "I met her two hours ago, Henry. I haven't fallen for her. I think she's beautiful. That's all. I don't even know her yet."

"But you think she's gonna stay, and everything is going to be wonderful with her, don't you?"

Donald didn't answer right away, prompting Henry to lean forward slightly, raising his eyebrows.

"Don't you?" he repeated.

Donald nodded and shrugged. "I reckon I do.

She seemed like the kind of woman who can be trusted. She's no shrew. I could tell."

Henry narrowed his eyes and gave Donald a soft punch on the arm. "You know, I've always trusted your opinion, buddy. I think you have a good sense of other people. You got good intuition, you know. If you think this lady is going to work out and save us from a fate of Buster and Conrad, I'm gonna hope for that, too."

Donald grinned at him. It felt good for his foreman to treat him as an equal and as a friend.

"You gonna show me what I still need to do in this shed or not?" he asked, gesturing to the building in the distance with his head.

Henry laughed. "Yeah. Come on. It's not gonna take you long to figure out what we need to do."

"I'm sure it won't."

Donald followed Henry toward the shed, thinking he wouldn't be able to really get any quality work done until he found out what the result of Aileen's meeting with Lionel was. He was glad he hadn't had to keep pretending to be Lionel any longer.

Now he could only hope Aileen accepted him as Donald.

12

Aileen left the office feeling like she'd stepped into a different world. When she'd asked for a change in her life, she didn't know it would be so... strange.

Lionel told her to go explore. He made sure to tell her she was not a prisoner and had free rein to go wherever she wanted, including back to the stagecoach station, where she would be taken home at no charge to her.

Aileen didn't want to leave, though. Her half-hour in Lionel's office had made an impact on her she hadn't expected.

Then again, she hadn't expected any of this, had she?

As she walked away from the office, she

wondered how she should act around Donald. He'd seemed so nice and sweet. Every strange thing she'd experienced that morning was explained. She got the impression he hadn't told Donald very much, which was why the young man looked so nervous when he picked her up and during the marriage ceremony.

The scent of food cooking met her nose. It was early afternoon, and she wasn't expecting that. Despite the food she'd eaten a few hours ago, her stomach rumbled when her nose filled with the smell of meat.

She hurried toward the kitchen. As nervous as she was to be in a new place, she had never been shy and was determined to make this her home as quickly as possible.

She pushed the door to the kitchen open, quietly wondering where Donald was. It seemed to her that both of them had been Lionel's pawns. Having something in common with someone else here was a good way to start a friendship, she thought.

There were two ladies in the kitchen with Mary.

Mary's eyes lit up when she saw Aileen. The conversation the three women had been having ended abruptly when they saw her.

She smiled at them, hoping she didn't look anxious.

"Good afternoon," she said. "I'm Aileen." She went in, holding her hand out to the woman dressed as a cook, with a large, long apron slung around her waist and around her neck. She was a tall woman and looked very strong. She reminded Aileen of a butcher back in Boston she used to go to for pieces of meat.

"Irene," the woman said. "This is Belle and Mary."

"We've met," Mary interjected, stepping forward. Aileen was a little surprised by how delighted the young woman looked. "You've decided to stay, haven't you? Oh, I just knew you would. It was so smart for Mr. McArthur to send Donald. He's such a gentleman and so good-looking."

Aileen was stunned when the maid threw herself at her and hugged her tight.

"All right, Mary, that's enough. You're gonna scare the woman off." It was the third woman, Belle , who spoke up, laughter in her voice. Aileen looked at her as Mary pulled away with a little giggle of her own. "She's just really happy, Aileen. We all are. Oh, is it all right if we call you that? Or should we call you Mrs. McArthur?"

Aileen shook her head. "Aileen is fine. I'm surprised by how happy everyone is to have me here. I know I've only met you three and Donald and Lionel, but I don't think I've ever felt more welcome anywhere before." Even though she was basically kidnapped, she thought with an internal giggle. "None of you even know me."

"There's a very good reason for that," Irene answered, turning back to her stove, and poking at a large piece of meat in a pot with a large, pronged fork. "I don't know how the men feel, but we have been dreading the day Conrad and Buster get their hands on this estate. We've been talking about it amongst ourselves for a long time now. We don't want them here. We don't ever want them here."

She sounded a little frightened. Aileen shook her head. "I am shocked that anyone raised by Lionel would end up that way."

"Those boys are older than you, my dear," Irene continued, glancing over her shoulder. "They aren't boys anymore. They were teenagers when he married their mother. I wasn't here, thank the Lord. None of us were here when they were young."

Aileen nodded in understanding. "Oh, so they already had their personalities set."

"Yes. Conrad is the younger one. He was twelve

when they came to live here. Buster was fifteen. Conrad is the better of the two. He had just enough influence from Mr. McArthur to form at least some kind of personality that wasn't horse manure."

Aileen chuckled. She took a seat at the tall table in the middle of the room and watched as Irene added salt and seasoning to the meat she was cooking.

"Will you tell me about the people here?" she asked. "Does everyone know I'm married to Lionel?"

"I don't know what the men know," Irene said. "But Mr. McArthur told us all at the beginning of his campaign to find a wife exactly what he was doing."

"That was a nice night," Belle said wistfully, sitting back in her chair. "He provided such a nice dinner for us all. He had Donald go into town and get us all food from the restaurant, and he brought it back here."

"So Donald knew about it?"

"I really don't think he did," Belle said, tilting her head to the side. "Now that I think about it, I don't think Mr. McArthur told anybody what he was doing but us ladies. I don't even think Jonah knows."

Aileen nodded. "Donald tried to tell me who worked here, but I think he was too nervous to really think straight."

Irene laughed softly. "That boy. He is so sweet."

"Donald isn't a boy," Mary said in a voice that revealed she was infatuated with the ranch hand. She sat forward, a dreamy look on her face.

"He's off-limits, dearie," Irene said, shaking her spatula at the young maid. "Don't you get any thoughts in your head."

"Why is he off limits?" Aileen asked. She was very curious to know the reason behind that. She wasn't going to be married to Lionel forever. Donald seemed like a better prospect than most, considering she was already married to him.

Irene gestured to Belle with her head. "Belle here will show you around in a bit. After I've got some food in your belly. You're a tiny little thing, aren't you? You need to eat."

Aileen was pleasantly taken aback. She had never in her life considered herself to be a "tiny little thing," but compared to the tall, robust stature of Irene, she could see why the cook would say that. She gave the woman a grin.

"I am grateful for that, thank you. But please tell me why Donald is off-limits?"

Irene and the maids shared looks that Aileen didn't understand.

"Donald is a gentleman," Irene said. "He is good

on his own merits. But Mr. McArthur gives him a little more attention than the rest of the men. It's not that Donald is exactly off-limits. It's just that no one wants to get involved with him knowing they will be fired from their job if Donald gets angry with them."

Aileen frowned. "What? How can Donald have that much power? That is wrong. He shouldn't be—"

"She didn't word that right," Mary cut into Aileen's questioning. The maid bit her bottom lip and glanced at the cook. "I'm sorry, Irene. Aileen, let me take you and show you what she means. You'll understand if I tell you what's really going on. You can't be expected to understand unless you see for yourself."

Aileen graciously accepted the cold-cut meat sandwich Irene handed to her and drank several swallows of orange juice before she ate it. She did so in a hurry, wanting to leave with Mary and find out what was actually happening with Donald and Lionel. She had given her hand to Donald, even if Lionel was the one who had signed the certificate and given her his name.

13

Her stomach satisfactorily full, Aileen waited by the door for Mary to finish her bowl of grits. The girl was standing and scraping up the last bits before she hurried over to Aileen with a sheepish smile, tapping a napkin around her mouth.

"You look very anxious," Mary said.

Aileen nodded. "I'd like to know what's going on. That's all. I'm very curious."

Mary gave her a nod of her own. "I can see that. Come with me."

She went through the door and down the hall back to the front of the house. Aileen was surprised by how hard her heart was beating. She had yet to get any negative feelings from being in the house, and even with this strange mystery Mary was about to solve for her, she was still more excited and interested than anything else.

Mary stopped abruptly and looked up above a massive stone fireplace in the foyer underneath the spiraling staircase that led to the second floor. Aileen turned her eyes to see what Mary was looking at.

Her jaw dropped, and her eyes widened. The magnificent painting was a beautiful rendition of Donald. He was in a smart business suit that looked very outdated. Aileen quickly realized it wasn't a picture of Donald. It had to be an ancestor from a hundred years ago or so.

"I thought that was Donald at first."

Mary nodded. "That's why Mr. McArthur treats him the way he does."

"They are related? If they are related, how come Lionel isn't leaving the estate to Donald?"

"They aren't related," Mary remarked. Aileen looked at the maid, who was staring at her, probably to see her reaction. She lifted both eyebrows.

"But how can that be? This man looks very much like Donald. I thought it was him."

"I know. You said. But it's not Donald, and they aren't related. This is a portrait of the late Alexander

McArthur. He was Lionel's father. None of us working here now knew him when he was alive... well, maybe Henry does. He's been here the longest. The foreman."

"So Donald isn't even the foreman?" Aileen was surprised by that. She looked at the portrait again, amazed by how close the resemblance was. Donald could easily have been this man's son. Or twin brother.

"No, Henry was already foreman when he came. Mr. McArthur made Donald second foreman."

Aileen nodded, remembering Donald mentioning there was a foreman and a second. She went through their conversation on the way home and decided Donald had been very clever when he covered up for his boss the way he did.

"It seems like everyone here really likes being here," she said softly, her eyes remaining on the picture just because it looked so much like Donald, and she felt like she was married to the man.

"We do. Mr. McArthur is great to work for. He's real generous." She leaned over to whisper dramatically. "We were really hoping you wouldn't turn out to be a hateful woman. We don't want that for Mr. McArthur. He's a sweet old man, and we like him."

"I can tell."

"Come on, let me show you around some more."

"So it's because Lionel thinks so much of Donald that you all consider him to be off-limits?"

When Mary responded, it was in a nonchalant tone. She waved one hand in the air as she spoke. "Oh, Donald isn't a flirtatious man anyway. I mean, he is blind to it. Whenever we give him a compliment, he blushes and kicks the dirt. He doesn't know how to respond to it. You can't find a woman if you can't be assertive enough to flirt. Don't you agree?"

Aileen had never thought about it, but she nodded in agreement anyway.

"I know Belle has tried to flirt with him at least a few times over the years."

Aileen had a feeling Mary was throwing the other maid under the cart. She suspected it was actually Mary who had that long-standing infatuation.

"Is that so?" she asked.

Mary nodded. "He's just... I wouldn't say shy. He's sweet. Reserved. A hard worker, though. I've taken food out to the men a few times, and I'm glad I don't have to do that stuff. I wouldn't last a day."

Aileen agreed with her. "I've seen that myself. I'll work in the house any day."

Mary gazed at her as they went up the steps. "You work? You don't come from a privileged family?"

Aileen brought her eyebrows together. "No. I was a companion for a wealthy young lady, though, and they treated me like family, so I feel like I do."

Mary nodded. "Mr. McArthur told us he was sending for a lady to marry to prevent his stepsons from getting the estate. He didn't say where he was finding her or anything like that. We never asked. Not our business, you know."

Aileen gave the young woman a pleasant grin. "I understand. No, I have never been wealthy before. I think that will work out well for you all in the end, though. I know what you're going through and how hard you've worked to get where you are. I won't let anyone take that away from you. No matter what. Whether Lionel is still here or not. I've given him my promise."

"How many letters... this is your room here, by the way... how many letters did you two send each other?"

"I sent him two letters, the first one and the one accepting his invitation. He sent me one after I answered the ad."

"You must have wanted to get here really fast. No trouble at home, I hope?"

"No, not at all. I just felt it was time for a change. I'd been thinking about it for a long time." She paused reflectively. "There was something about Lionel's ad that got my attention. It wasn't long and didn't have a lot of details to it. It just caught my eye, and I really felt like this was the one I was supposed to answer."

"So you did answer an ad." Mary gave a satisfactory nod. "I thought so. We were trying to figure that out earlier when we saw Donald bring you in."

"He didn't know you knew about Lionel's plan, did he?" Aileen asked.

Mary shook her head, putting one hand up to her mouth, so her fingers were on her smiling lips. "He was so surprised when you both came in. I just know he expected me to call him by his name."

"You almost did," Aileen replied with a laugh of her own.

"You caught that. Oh, how embarrassing."

Aileen looked around the room, taking her attention away from the maid to see where she would be living. It was huge with a door on either side of the room, glass double doors that led out to a veranda, and two huge windows flanking the doors.

"Oh my," she murmured. A four-poster bed with black and white bedclothes sat to her right. It was the biggest bed she'd ever slept in. "This is amazing. Did you decorate?"

"I did." Mary sounded very proud of herself. "Belle was the one who did most of it, though. I can't take all the credit."

"Well, it's lovely. Those doors are for..." She pointed to the two of them.

"That one goes to your washroom. You have your own tub. There is running water in that room. You're lucky." Mary didn't sound jealous. She just smiled at Aileen. "That one is a large closet."

"A closet." Aileen was pleasantly surprised.

"Yes. I think you'll like it here. If you need anything at all, please don't hesitate to ask."

After the tour of the house, Aileen followed Mary outside. She immediately spotted Donald with the other men in front of the bunkhouse talking. Her heartbeat sped up.

"Look, there's Donald. That's Henry with him. And Trevor and Johnny." Mary lifted one hand when the men looked over at them and waved.

Aileen flushed to her roots. She didn't know why she was suddenly embarrassed, but she grabbed Mary and steered her away from the men. She could hear the men laughing behind her, ribbing Donald about having an "admirer".

Sometimes she wished her face didn't show every single thing she was thinking.

14

The next morning, Aileen awakened after a surprisingly peaceful night of sleep. Her very first thought was that she should go see if Theresa needed help with the children. She sat up and slid out of bed, shaking the sleep from her brain. It wasn't until she opened them and stretched her arms above her head that she remembered where she was.

The soft fabric draped over the posters of the bed brushed against her fingers when she stretched, and her eyes snapped open.

She looked around the large room and felt tiny in comparison. The beautiful pictures on the walls, the fresh flowers in the vases, it was all just so lovely.

She went through her morning routine thinking

about the Winchesters. The birthday bash they had thrown for her was magnificent and a lot of fun. They'd hired people to run games, strewn banners all over, covered the trees in balloons and streamers, and even hired an illusionist to entertain the crowd of people that showed up. They all knew Aileen was leaving, so they'd all taken time out of their day to tell her goodbye and wish her farewell.

They'd expressed their love for her adamantly before she got on the stagecoach.

Aileen was confident she could find that same kinship with the people at the McArthur ranch. It would just take time. Still, she missed her family more than she thought she would.

As she went down the steps to go to the kitchen for breakfast, she wondered if she could expect any help from Donald after Lionel passed on. She wouldn't be able to run the place by herself. Lionel had to know that, too. She hoped he put a provision in the will that if she needed help, Donald would be the one to do it. Or Henry. Without giving her a hassle about it.

She didn't know what to do to run a ranch. She barely knew how to act as a wealthy hostess of a gigantic ranch.

She'd met the groom and the housekeeper the

day before. Bertie seemed perfectly capable of taking care of things, and Aileen made sure she knew she was still in charge of all that. She wasn't a typical mistress of the house, and she let Bertie know that. She'd found Bertie to be fun, encouraging, and all smiles. That was becoming typical here on the McArthur ranch.

Lionel was not in the dining room when she went in. He'd been quiet at dinner the night before, and she was too shy to say anything, so she stayed silent, ate, and went up to bed. She sat at the table by herself, unsure if she was supposed to go and get food for herself or not. She could smell that it was cooking, but with Lionel not in the room, she didn't know what to do.

Thankfully, the door to the kitchen swung open, and Belle came through carrying a tray.

"Good morning, Miss Aileen. You're right on time. I was just bringing this out."

"Will Lionel be down this morning, Belle?"

"I don't think so. He rarely comes here for breakfast. He is usually served in his room or on his veranda. That's where he likes to eat."

"He doesn't leave the house much, does he?"

"No, he doesn't like to venture out in the world anymore. He says it's a dangerous place for an wealthy old man like him." Belle grinned. "His words."

Belle set the tray down and removed the top to reveal bacon, eggs, biscuits, a small jar of jam, and a large cup of orange juice. The maid smiled at her. "Irene says based on what you ate yesterday, she doesn't think you'll need more than this to fill you up."

"Oh, this is more than enough, thank you."

Belle nodded and turned to leave. Aileen felt a streak of anxiety pass through her, leaving her chest tight.

"Wait," she exclaimed, putting out one hand in a stop motion. Belle turned back with a look of surprise. "Can you stay with me for a while? I don't really want to be alone. I'll let Irene know if you already had work to do."

Belle looked mildly surprised but nodded. She took the seat at an angle to Aileen. "You're the boss now, Miss Aileen. Just like Lionel. He told us we were to listen to you."

"Did he really?" Aileen raised her eyebrows. "Before I even got here?"

The young maid shrugged her shoulders. "He told us he knew all he needed to know about you from your letter. He was sure you weren't going to be a terrible person."

"He took quite a chance."

Belle smiled wide. "That's how he's gotten so rich, though. He told us he has taken risks all his life, and for some reason, things just work out for him. We told him he was lucky, but he said he was blessed."

"After spending the first fifty years of his life rejecting love, he must feel blessed that he ever had it at all."

Belle shifted in the chair, turning her head to look outside. Her brown hair was piled high on her head, kept tight with many barrettes and pins. Her uniform was crisp and clean, which would be expected first thing in the morning if Aileen didn't distinctly remember Belle looking sharp in the late afternoon the day before.

The food was cooked to perfection. Aileen ate while Belle filled her in a little more on the workings of the ranch. She noticed that whenever the maid said anything about Lionel, her eyes would go soft, and her voice would lower.

"It seems like everyone working here feels like Lionel is their grandfather," she mentioned during a pause in their conversation. "He's really loved, isn't he?"

"He is," Belle replied, folding her arms over her ample chest and sitting back. "He tells everyone his story when he first hires them. I think to let them know they are getting the best of him and to be grateful because a lot of people got the worst of him for a very long time. When he told me, he said he's worked twice as hard for the last several decades to reimagine himself, to be nicer to people and not worry so much about making money."

"It seems to me that fifty years as a hard man would be difficult to undo."

"It's too much for some people," Belle admitted. "Too long. That's why he has no old friends, no one he trusts, no family other than all of us. We love him for who he is now and don't have to hold past grudges against him. That's all he needs, really. Someone who won't judge his cold, callous behavior of the past and make it seem like he's still like that."

"And about breakfast?"

"He lets us know with the bell system. It's beside his bed. He pulls the sash when he wakes up, and we have his breakfast to him a half-hour later. Or sooner, if it's ready."

"Does he wake at the same time every day?"

"Usually, yes."

At that moment, Mary came through the door, carrying another tray, interrupting Aileen's train of thought.

"Is that for Lionel?" Aileen asked.

"Yes. Would you like to take it up to him?"

"I would like that if you don't mind."

"He usually eats on the veranda. But if he's fallen asleep in his comfy chair, just leave it in the room. He'll see it when he wakes up."

"But won't it be cold by then?" Aileen was concerned. The maids gave her affectionate glances.

"He doesn't mind," Mary said.

Aileen didn't want him to eat cold food. She would have to make sure he started eating right from now on.

15

Later that afternoon, Aileen decided she would spend some time in the library. She had unpacked her things, toured the grounds, got to meet her horse, and take a ride, and spent lunch in the kitchen, eating with Irene and the girls.

As much as she loved reading, she'd put off going back to the library because she knew she wouldn't want to leave.

She'd come right after lunch, and it was three hours later. She was still looking through the books, having stopped and read several small portions of various books. A book on butterflies caught her interest. She'd spent at least an hour perusing that.

The library had three large chairs and one

couch. Two desks held stacks of books that people had apparently pulled down and not put back up. She wondered who it was reading all those books. She hadn't seen Lionel in there yet and doubted the help would leave things so unkempt. She didn't know if others had full access to everything Lionel owned like she did, either.

As she examined one of the stacks on the desk, she noticed a pattern. They were all medical journals. Someone was looking through for medical advice. Moving her eyes to the shelf directly to her right, she noticed they were all medical books, as well. There was one complete shelf that appeared to be dedicated to the topic.

Aileen set about reshelving the books that had been left out. It felt good to be doing something again. She didn't know how the very wealthy could stand just walking around not doing anything. How did they find things to fill their day without lifting a finger in work?

She didn't like feeling lazy. Aileen was going to help with whatever work needed to be done, and that wouldn't stop once she took over the ranch. If she saw something that only needed a simple fix and she knew how to do it, she wasn't calling any servants over. If she could do it herself, she would.

She jumped when the door to the library slammed open behind her. She spun around and stared at Donald, who was completely red in the face, one hand gripping the edge of the door.

"I am so sorry," he apologized sheepishly. "The door got away from me."

Aileen wished she had seen that happen. What she pictured in her mind made her burst out laughing. She slapped one hand over her mouth, turning as red as he was.

"I'm sorry for laughing," she said through her fingers. "I couldn't help it."

She noticed when his face drained of blood, and an easy smile came to his lips. "The boss wants to see us," he said, jerking one thumb over his shoulder. "You want to follow me?"

"I don't know," Aileen said, narrowing her eyes. She set down the book she was holding and crossed her arms over her chest. "The last time I followed you, I wound up in a place I never expected."

She made sure her voice was teasing so he would know she was amused and not upset.

He chuckled, shaking his head. "I have to apologize for that, Miss. I didn't know what was happening until that day, and, uh, I really have a lot of respect for Mr. McArthur. I don't like to let him down. He asked something of me, and I had to do it for him. I hope you understand."

Aileen nodded. She was glad to hear a gracious apology from him, even though she didn't need one.

"It's all right, Donald. I've had time to think about it, and I no longer want to kill you in your sleep."

Donald's eyes widened. He stared at her like he thought she was serious.

"I'm joking with you. I wouldn't do anything like that. I'm a Godfearing woman."

"I'm glad to hear you say that. I know I haven't known you long, but I had a feeling you would be good for this ranch as soon as I saw you."

He sounded so sincere, so genuine. Aileen looked at his face a little longer than usual, which made him turn his eyes away self-consciously. He really did look so much like Lionel's father. She was still surprised by it, and she hadn't looked at the painting since the day before.

Lionel's office was only two doors from the library. That was something Aileen would never forget. She put her hand on the doorknob, and a tingle went straight up her arm when he rested his hand over hers.

"You're the lady of the house," he said quietly,

looking her in the eye. "I need to be opening the door for you. Not the other way around. Allow me, ma'am."

She slid her hand out from under his. It burned from where he'd touched it for at least three seconds after they were no longer in contact. She covered that hand with the other one, never taking her eyes from his. He even turned the knob and pushed the door open without looking away from her.

"Donald!"

Lionel's voice barked the man's name, and Donald's eyes snapped to his boss.

"Yes, sir," he responded firmly, standing up straight, the look on his face hardening into seriousness.

"I've got to finish consulting with my lawyer here. You and Laura go fetch Henry. He needs to be here to see this, too."

Aileen's ears perked up when she heard the word lawyer. She leaned forward and saw two men and a woman in the room. They were sitting and standing around the office, leisurely, relaxed looks on their faces.

"Yes, sir." Donald nodded and closed the door. He looked at her. "Come on. Let's go get Henry."

"Who were those people in there?" Aileen asked. "Are those his stepsons in there?"

Aileen was slightly amused by the look of terror that passed over Donald's face. She was almost anxious to meet the stepsons that caused every employee of the ranch to recoil in horror.

Then again, maybe she didn't.

"No," he said bluntly. "They aren't in there. Thank God. Obnoxious men. Both of them." He shook his head.

"I don't think I've ever seen anyone cause such a reaction in people before. None of you like either of those men, do you?"

Donald shook his head. He opened the front door, and as he went out behind her, he put his hat on his head. "Nothing to like about them."

"Irene said no one working here now was here when they were here. When they lived here. Is that true? She seemed unsure about the ranch hands."

"Nope, not one of us was here when they were. Conrad is the younger one. He had just moved out when Henry came on board. He came back a lot there at the beginning, they both did. We've all gotten a chance to experience what that's like—to have them here trying to tell everyone what to do and change things and convince Mr. McArthur to do things he doesn't want to do." He snorted. "Mostly sign over property to them or give them money. Scoundrels." He spat on the ground beside him as they stepped off the last step.

"I don't think I want to meet them," Aileen remarked softly.

"You don't. Trust me."

Aileen glanced over at him. She'd been on the McArthur ranch a little over 24 hours and was in the predicament of a lifetime. No matter what happened, she was in for a fight. The evil brothers were sure to wreak havoc after Lionel's death.

Aileen was about to ask Donald if he planned to help her run the ranch when the time came when he yelled out Henry's name and started walking faster.

She stayed back, watching him retrieve the foreman, thinking about how handsome he was.

16

In the office, ten minutes later, Donald watched as the man he knew to be Mr. McArthur's lawyer got up to let Aileen sit down.

"Thank you for coming in to see me, Aileen. You look delightful."

"Thank you, Lionel," Aileen replied.

He gave Donald a quick glance and a nod before returning his gaze to Aileen's beautiful face. Donald was always surprised by how attractive he found her to be. He'd stumbled going in the library, falling against the door and making it slam open, but when he looked at Aileen standing there putting books back on shelves, his heart did what his feet had just done. He was breathless, taking in her beauty.

Now, he found that beauty distracting. He dragged his eyes from her face and listened to what his boss had to say.

"You already know these people, Donald. Aileen, this is my lawyer, Mark Handelburg. One of the most trusted men with money that money can buy." He grinned. The lawyer bent at the waist and took hold of Aileen's fingers, briefly. "This is my doctor, Jean St. Pierre. You can call him Doc Jean. That's how we do it here in America, isn't that right, Doc?"

The doctor was a small man Donald had always thought looked like the country he came from. He had a French accent that was thick but didn't keep his words from being understandable. He also took Aileen's hand but kissed the top of it.

"And this is my beloved secretary, Anne Ross. She has been with me for almost fifteen years, haven't you, my dear? Since she was a young girl trying to make a little money. You and your family don't have to worry about that anymore, do you?"

Anne, whom Donald had always thought was the perfect secretary for Lionel because of her punctuality, straightforwardness, and intelligence, gave Aileen a brilliant smile. She was clutching ledgers to her chest, which was how Donald always thought of her because she did that particular pose so often.

She took a few steps forward, and the women shook hands.

"Now that we are all introduced, I'll tell you why we're here. I am going to make sure those two monsters don't get my money. Everyone in this room is aware of the problem and has been made aware of my solution. Aileen, Mark would like to ask you a few questions."

Donald watched Aileen's face. She looked unperturbed.

"That's fine," she said, turning in the chair slightly, so she was facing the lawyer.

"You are here of your own free will, is that correct?" he asked.

Aileen nodded. "Yes, I am."

"Do you have plans to take revenge against Lionel for bringing you here under false pretenses?"

Donald almost laughed. If she was planning to, would she tell him?

Apparently, Aileen had the same thought because she chuckled softly, glancing at Lionel and shaking her head. "No, of course not."

"Do you trust that he has your best interests at heart?"

"I do think so, yes."

"And lastly, do you feel you have been kidnapped or taken prisoner?"

Aileen shook her head. "No, not at all."

The rest of the group looked satisfied with her answers. Donald watched Lionel push a folder across his desk toward Aileen. The old man looked up at him.

"This is for you, too, Donald. Come over here."

Donald went closer to the desk but stayed a respectful distance back. Lionel gave him a frustrated look and waved his hand.

"What are you doing? Get over here. You need to read through this, too. I want your signature on this document as a witness."

Donald blinked at the man. What was going on? What was the document he was signing? Was he marrying Aileen, after all?

He wished.

He leaned over and read the document Lionel pulled out of the folder and slid in front of him. A different document was given to Aileen. He didn't notice at first, but Henry got a third piece of paper and was reading it in front of the window.

Chills covered Donald's body when he read what was written there. It was a consent to take a twenty-five percent share of the business after Lionel passed away. Part of the ranch would be his.

Donald immediately felt unworthy. He knew why the old man was giving this to him, why he was so generous. It was then that he noticed Henry had a paper that looked an awful lot like his. He must be the person with the majority share unless Lionel was giving it to all three of them.

"You three will be running my business when I'm gone," Lionel said firmly, wagging one long finger between them. "Aileen will be in charge. Henry, you and Donald will take care of running things she doesn't and can't do. I believe the three of you will make sure the ranch, the business, and the staff are kept safe from Conrad and Buster. Am I right to believe that?"

"Yes, sir," the men answered at the same time.

Aileen's "Yes, Lionel," was in that blend of voices, as well.

Lionel sat forward, giving them a serious look, one at a time. "I am counting on you. My doctor, Anne, Mark, they will be witnesses to this will I have drawn up. These are attachments to the will saying that the three of you consent to take the estate between the three of you. If you didn't notice, there is also a portion of that document that says you will resist any and all attempts by my stepsons to gain access to my property. I would rather this ranch house burn down than see them live one more day in it."

"We won't let them get it," Henry stated firmly. He brought the paper over to the desk, leaned over, and held out his hand. Lionel gave him the fountain pen, and they all watched as he signed the paper. "I won't let them anywhere near this place, sir," he added, slapping the fountain pen down on the paper. A tiny bit of ink dripped from the end when he did that, making a small dot on the paper he'd signed.

Without hesitation, Aileen leaned over and picked up the pen. Seeing that she was also on board helped Donald make up his mind. There was little doubt to begin with, though. He wanted to do whatever he could for his boss. He waited until Aileen had signed her name at the bottom of her paper in front of her. As soon as she set the pen down, he picked it up and signed his own.

The three of them waved the papers in the air while the conversation resumed.

Donald watched the others talking, thinking how strange it felt to be in what might as well have been an arranged marriage. By signing these documents and being put in Lionel's will with Aileen, he was essentially signing another marriage license. He was already fake married to her. The longer she stayed, the closer Lionel was pushing them together.

He certainly didn't have a problem with that. He had stepped away from the desk to get a better look at everything going on and watched while the lawyer, doctor, and secretary signed the new will. It left everything to Aileen, all controlling power to her, with the codicils that Henry and Donald were also getting part of the company but would answer to her. Donald wasn't told anything else that was in the will, but he was betting there were provisions for everyone who worked at the ranch.

The whole meeting took about an hour, and the group stayed a little longer to talk. Henry came over to chat with him, but he barely caught everything his foreman was saying because his mind was distracted by the beautiful woman talking to the secretary Anne Ross across the room.

The ladies were standing in front of the window now and the sunlight beaming through caught Aileen's red hair, making it gleam. It formed a halo around her, a vision of beauty that made Donald's heart thump in his chest. He couldn't wait to get out of there and talk to her.

17

———

Lionel asked Aileen to stay and talk to him for a moment before she left the office after the meeting. She willingly obliged and only turned to see when Donald went out. She was numb, unable to believe what had just happened. In the last hour, she had officially become an extremely wealthy woman.

She didn't feel any different.

"Are you happy here, Aileen?" Lionel asked. "I know it's only a short while, but I need to know that you are not unhappy."

"I'm feeling fine, Lionel," she responded. "Thank you for asking."

"I hope that we will soon be able to have some

time to talk. I apologize that I haven't been more available to you."

"It's all right. I understand."

"I just wanted you to know that if you need anything, I am here for you. My door is always open."

"Thank you."

She got to her feet and walked to the door. Once there, she turned back to look at him. "I appreciate all you've done, Lionel. I must say I am very surprised you would trust a stranger with your entire life's fortune. But if you're going to trust anyone with it, I'm glad it's me. I won't let you down."

When Lionel smiled at her, she felt a warm wave of affection wash through her.

She stepped outside and almost ran into Donald, who was standing there idly, apparently doing nothing. She narrowed her eyes at him.

"Were you listening at the door, Mr. Ferris?" she demanded.

He looked regretful. "No, ma'am. I was waiting for you. Just wanted to see if you were willing to have a chat with me."

She surveyed his face, realizing that all she wanted to do at that moment was have a chat with him.

"You aren't too busy?" she asked.

He shook his head. "No, ma'am. You are the boss. I always have time for you."

Aileen didn't know how to feel about that. She'd never been treated like a boss before. "I was thinking I might want some time alone." She kept her voice low, moving her eyes past Donald to the front door at the end of the hall. She didn't want time alone now. That had been a fleeting thought. All she wanted to do now was give her attention to the man standing in front of her.

"Are you sure?" He sounded a little urgent.

She returned her eyes to his face and was taken in by how attractive he was. "No, I think it would be best if we did have a chat. I think maybe we have a lot to talk about. It looks like we've been made business partners, whether we like it or not."

His face relaxed when he smiled. She admired his eyes and dropped her eyes to his lips when he spoke. "I don't know about you, but I don't have a problem with it. I'm actually real surprised he did that. I'm only the second foreman here."

Aileen nodded. "I saw the portrait above the fireplace under the spiral stairs. You look just like his father. It's not a wonder that he treats you special."

Donald looked like he didn't know how to

respond to that. He touched her arm, sending a tingle over her skin, and said, "I'll go tell Henry we're going to talk."

For a moment, Aileen was afraid he was going to ask Henry to join them. She refrained from telling him she just wanted the two of them to talk. She liked Henry. But she wanted to get to know the man she had married, even if it wasn't a real marriage. For some reason, the act of saying I do and hearing it from Donald's mouth formed a bond in her mind that she couldn't shake. She'd immediately accepted that he was her husband from the moment she saw him in the station.

Yes, it had been because he was so alluring. But as time went on, Aileen was beginning to realize that he was a man worth marrying. It was early yet, but she had a feeling he was exactly what he portrayed himself to be. A hard-working gentleman with a good heart.

She stood on the front porch watching while he jogged over to Henry, who had gone back to the bunkhouse steps and was talking to Trevor.

Shouldn't she be at least a little upset about what had happened to her? She'd been deceived from the moment she stepped foot in Gustaf's Corner at the stagecoach station. She should be up there packing up her stuff. She should never have unpacked in the first place.

Somehow, there wasn't an angry bone in her body. In fact, she wanted to laugh at herself for her silly thoughts.

To her mind, Lionel's actions were justified. Maybe another woman wouldn't have seen it that way. But Aileen was looking to create a new life for herself, and so far, McArthur Ranch was proving to be the perfect spot to do that. Donald's only mistake so far had been revealing he was capable of deception. But what honest person wasn't willing to stretch things a little bit to help out a good friend? And how had she really been hurt? No one had been hurt, as far as she could see. She'd wanted adventure. That's what she was getting.

Plus, a future owning the ranch, shared with Donald, and gaining all the assets Lionel had accumulated over his long life wasn't exactly a prison sentence.

Donald was coming back to her, and she stepped to the end of the porch, slowly taking the steps down to meet him.

"You want to ride? I can get the horses ready. Or maybe you'd rather take a walk by the creek."

She smiled at him. "Let's walk by the creek. It's

not too hot for that. The water will help keep us cool."

"That sounds just fine, Miss." He held out his arm to her. "I mean, Mrs. I apologize."

She wrapped her hands around his elbow and walked beside him, smiling up at him. They crossed the front lawn and went down the slightly sloping hill to the creek.

"I saw this creek from the road when you were bringing me here," she said. "I still can't get over how beautiful this land is. Did you have anything to do with that?"

She was curious but not surprised when he shook his head. He sounded flattered when he responded.

"I had nothing to do with it, unfortunately. I don't work these grounds at all. That's the landscapers that do that. I work in the field with the cows and horses."

"I think it's beautiful," Aileen murmured. She couldn't get enough of the visions she saw before her.

"That's because it is."

"Do you know anything about the history of this place?" she asked.

Again, he shook his head, and she was a little

more disappointed than she had been. "Oh, that's too bad," she said.

"Maybe there's something about the history in the library," Donald mentioned. "You find the book, and I promise I'll read it. Then we can discuss the history of McArthur Ranch."

She smiled at him. "I like that idea. Good thinking. That will give us something else to do together."

Aileen blushed, her fingers tightening around his strong arm. She felt him flex, and it made her stomach nervous. She wanted to push herself closer to him but didn't out of respect. She didn't want to make him uncomfortable.

"I've been wanting to ask you something, Donald," she said, keeping her voice smooth and calm. He looked at her with an inquisitive look on his handsome face. "Although I think Lionel covered it, really. I was thinking about how much help I would need making sure the business stays running, and the ranch is run the way it's always been. Lionel had both you and Henry sign your lives over to me, basically. I hope that's all right. I know I can count on you to help me run the ranch." She hesitated, looking at him. "Right?"

"Of course," he responded. "Henry and I aren't going anywhere."

"You promise? You won't sell your part to the brothers?"

Donald looked at her under hooded eyelids. "Aileen. I signed a paper saying I wouldn't. I pledged my loyalty to Lionel. I married a woman under false pretenses for him. Do you think I'd let his awful stepsons get anywhere near his property once he's gone?"

Aileen smiled at him.

"I'm so glad to hear that."

18

---

onald was thrilled to be walking next to Aileen, talking like they were old friends. He could already tell she would make an excellent business partner.

It was a little funny that she would question his loyalty to Lionel when she was the one who had been there all of two days. He had been there ten years. The smile she gave him expressed no malice on her part, so he didn't berate her for not trusting him. The two of them were still strangers, and they would need time to get to know each other better.

"Can I ask you something?" Aileen asked as they walked along the small shore of the creek.

"Of course," he responded. He was actually anxious for her to ask him questions. He wanted to tell her anything she wanted to know. The paper he'd signed made him feel like they'd gotten married a second time. Each time got better, he thought with a smile.

"What can you tell me about Henry? I haven't even really talked with the man. How does he feel about my being here? And Lionel willing his estate to me. I know Henry gets a portion but still... what do you think he's thinking? Is he angry with me?"

Donald's eyebrows shot up. "Angry with you? Why would he be?"

"I would think after being in one job for that long, one might expect a little more than a small settlement in the will, even if it is a portion of the business."

"Henry doesn't expect anything. He has a house and a family and a life outside this ranch. Mr. McArthur knows I don't. He knows this is my home."

"It's hard to believe you look so much like his father. How do you think that happened? You're sure you aren't related?"

"We aren't," Donald replied, shaking his head. "It's probably a good thing we're not."

Aileen tilted her head to the side, making her red hair shift over her shoulders. Her green eyes were curious. "Why do you say that?"

Donald hesitated, forming the right words so he wouldn't insult his boss. "Because he's told me about his past. He... wasn't as nice to people as he could have been. He told me he pushed away his parents and siblings, and any other relatives. If I'd known him back then, I might not be as forgiving now. Plus, I would personally be someone else, raised different, all that. I'm glad I am who I am."

"Well, I told you all about me yesterday." She smiled up at him. "Tell me a little about you."

Donald felt his cheeks flush. He glanced down at her. "Why would you want to know anything about me?"

She pursed her lips and narrowed her eyes at him. "I just told you. You know about me. Now it's my turn. So tell me. Do you have your parents? Are they here? Any family? Never married, right?"

Donald laughed, amused by her rapid-fire questions. "I don't know if I can remember everything you just asked, but I'll tell you about my family. I was raised in Jacksontown, Oklahoma. I have two sisters and two brothers, but my brothers died of influenza when they were little. My sisters are older than me. My father was in a mining accident when I was in my teens, and my mother died right after him. I think... we all think she died of a broken heart."

"I'm so sorry to hear that," Aileen said sympathetically. "You've been touched by a lot of death, haven't you?"

Donald shrugged. "Within my family? Yes. But it happens."

"And you still have your sisters, don't you?"

Donald thought about Suzie and Sandy. "Yeah," he said in a plain voice. "I reckon I do."

She looked up at him. "Well, don't sound so enthusiastic about it. Don't you get along with them?"

"I guess," Donald could feel he was about to go on the defensive. "They are very... overprotective, you might say. I can hardly do anything when they are around without some form of critique or caution."

"I guess that must be hard to take," Aileen said with a nod, "still, who wouldn't want big sisters to protect them from the monsters."

Donald raised his eyebrows. He didn't want to say his big sisters *were* the monsters, though that was what went through his head.

"The rest of the crew don't like it when they come to visit," he said. "They are all over me, making sure everything is perfect for me. I would rather they stay away. I can take the birthday and Christmas cards without them being here to hover over me."

"I think that's cute."

He turned his eyes toward her without moving his head. "You won't when you meet them. You'll see what I mean."

"Will I?" Aileen sounded excited. He didn't know how he could explain to her that she really didn't want to meet Suzie and Sandy. She should just let sleeping dogs lie.

"I don't know. Maybe you will. Maybe you won't. I'm not inviting them here anytime soon. The next time they'll be here is for my wedding."

Aileen's eyes snapped to his face. "Are you supposed to be getting married?"

A chill ran over him. He felt guilty like he'd said something wrong and desperately needed to make it right. "No," he said quickly. "No, I have no plans to get married."

"You don't have a sweetheart then?"

He shook his head. He wondered if she was asking because she felt the way he did—attracted. It would be nice if she was. He made up his mind that he would see Lionel after his walk with Aileen and ask him how he was supposed to handle all this. If anyone had some sage advice for him, it would be Lionel.

He was about to continue their conversation by switching the topic when movement in the bushes caught his eye.

He grabbed her arm and made her stop walking. She looked at him in alarm.

"What is it?" she asked.

He shook his head at her but said nothing. His heart pounded as he calculated in his head where they must be on the McArthur property. They were on the west side of the property. Near the bull. Had he escaped? And if so, how did he do it this time?

"We need to go back in the other direction," he murmured, pulling her elbow sharply so that she cried out a little. "I'm sorry. Come on. Slowly. Back off. Just back away."

He took a few slow steps back, keeping his eyes on the area where he'd seen and heard the leaves rustling.

"What is it?" Aileen whispered loudly, her voice cracking and squeaking.

He glanced down at her. "It's that dang bull again. I just know it. He got out. You want to—"

He didn't get out the rest of his warning. The bull came barreling out of the bushes and slid to a stop near the water, making a cloud of dust rise in the air around his feet.

"Oh no," Aileen murmured breathlessly.

"Just stay calm," Donald said in a low voice, lifting one arm in front of her as if that would stop the bull. He took another step back, and his arm made her take the same step. "Slowly. We back off very slowly."

"I am, I am." There was no reason for her to repeat the words, but Donald understood. She was trying to comfort herself by latching onto the phrase.

"I'll keep you safe, Aileen. Don't you worry about a thing."

He sounded a lot more confident than he felt.

19

———

The bull stared at them. Donald stared back. He kept moving her backward, taking his time, trying to keep her calm. He knew she had to be scared out of her mind. The last thing anyone wanted was for Aileen to be mauled by that bull the day after coming to Gustaf's Corner. From the way she talked, the Winchester family would probably take a quick ride up there to skin his hide.

His heart slammed in his chest. He was relieved when he heard Henry's loud voice calling out.

"Oh, thank the Lord," Aileen whispered.

They weren't out of danger yet, though. The bull, though it seemed to perk up a bit hearing its name being called out, was still advancing slowly on them.

He seemed curious more than aggressive, which Donald wasn't used to. Normally, the animal would have charged by now.

"Why is it just looking at us?" she whispered.

"I don't know," he said over his shoulder. "Maybe he thinks you're pretty."

Aileen gasped quietly and slapped him softly on the back from where she was hiding behind him. She peeked around him, making him chuckle despite the danger they were in.

"Make it go away," she hissed frantically.

He scoffed at her. "How am I supposed to do that? I don't speak the language of bull."

"Well, I don't know. I'm not a bull expert, you know. I can handle screaming toddlers but not a thousand-pound bull."

"Oh, I don't know if he weighs that much." Donald appreciated the lighthearted tone she was using and responded with the same humor.

"He weighs enough to crush our bones," Aileen wailed as quietly as she could.

"Henry's on his way. I'm sure the others are, too, just hold your—"

He stopped speaking when the bull snorted, blowing air from its nose and lowering its head.

"Uh oh," Donald said quickly.

"What? Why are you saying uh oh? What's going on?"

Donald backed up another step, almost losing his balance because she was right behind him. She kept him from falling and stepped back herself.

"He's coming," Donald said out of the corner of his mouth. "Look out. He's coming. He's getting ready to charge."

"What is Henry going to do? Look at that thing."

"I see it, Aileen," Donald replied sarcastically. He moved back another few steps. The bull began to scrape one foot on the ground, a sure sign he was getting ready to run right for them. He lowered his head again and then bobbed it up and down.

Donald let out a high-pitched sound at the back of his throat but kept it as low-key as possible. His breathing was becoming rapid. He looked around for a weapon, any type of weapon, even a big rock. He glanced behind him and saw that Aileen had her knees bent, was holding a fairly large rock for a girl her size, and was rocking from side to side, looking like she was about to hurl that rock right at the monster that was stalking them.

He was really beginning to hate that bull.

They backed up together a few more paces, and he felt something hard under him. He glanced down and saw a fallen branch as thick as his arm. He slowly bent down and picked it up, shaking off the dirt, never taking his eyes from the animal.

The bull began rocking forward and back, snorting and huffing. Donald prepared himself to hit the animal as hard as he could with the branch.

Just as it looked like the bull was about to charge them, something flew through the air past Donald's head. Aileen had thrown the rock. It zipped through the air with much more speed than Donald would have expected. He watched in amazement as the rock smacked dead center in between the bull's eyes.

The animal grunted. Its eyes crossed, and it fell to the side, creating a huge cloud of dust around its enormous body.

Right at that moment, Henry and several ranch hands came bursting from the woods around them, cheering Aileen.

"I just barely got to see that amazing feat, Miss Aileen," Henry called out, a huge smile on his face. "I've never wanted to shoot an animal more, but this one don't belong to me, so I'm glad we didn't have to kill it."

"I don't know," Donald responded in a loud voice, "it might be dead. You see that shot? If that had been a bullet, no way that animal would be alive right now."

He watched as Henry and the other men came down to where they were and patted Aileen on the shoulder, complimenting her excellent arm.

"Can't hang around here, boys," Henry said. "Let's tie up this beast and get him back to his pen."

Donald watched them return to the unconscious bull before turning to her.

"Let's go on back. We can talk some more on the way. But if there's anything you really wanted to talk about or ask me, go ahead and do it now."

Aileen gazed at him, her green eyes drinking in his spirit. He didn't want to go back to work. He wanted to stay with Aileen for the rest of the day. And the night and the next day.

He held in a sigh. He didn't want her to think he was upset with her.

She shook her head. "I don't have any questions for you. I'm still getting used to this new place. And that..." She glanced behind them. "Was more excitement than I've had for a long time. I think right now I'd like to go take a nap."

"I'll walk you to your room."

"Thank you."

TWENTY MINUTES LATER, Donald was knocking on Lionel's office door.

"Come in."

He opened the door to see that Lionel was stretching out on the couch instead of being behind his desk. He had one arm over his eyes and turned his head to peek out at Donald from behind it as soon as he entered the room.

"Ah. Donald, my boy. How are you today?"

"I'm fine, Mr. McArthur. Thank you for asking."

"You really must call me Lionel, Donald. I am giving you part of my company after all."

"If you want me to. I don't know if I can get used to that after ten years, though."

"I'm sure you'll find a way. You won't have to for long anyway."

Donald felt remorse slide through him. "Do you really think you're going to... to..."

"To die soon?" Lionel finished the sentence for him, sitting up and swinging his legs around the front. "Yes, son. It's inevitable. I have foreseen it, and it will be soon."

Donald didn't want him to die. He wanted him to live on for a lot longer. "But you're only eighty.

You could live to be over a hundred for all you know."

Lionel laughed pleasantly. He shook one finger in Donald's direction. "I knew there was a reason I liked you. Actually, there are many reasons. Come on in here and sit down, son. Why are you still standing there?"

Donald felt a little foolish and went to one of the chairs to sit.

"Did you have something you wished to discuss with me?"

"I just wanted to ask you something, sir."

Lionel nodded, giving him a questioning look, raising his white eyebrows and making more wrinkles in his forehead.

"I'm going to be spending a lot of time with Aileen, I think," he said, pushing himself to get the words out before he chickened out. "And I don't want to disrespect you. She is married to you. I don't want to make you look bad in front of your employees."

Lionel shook his head. "Bertie and Henry have been told to tell their crew all about this, son. The ladies in the house already knew. They have been instructed not to think badly of you or Aileen for spending time together."

Donald was relieved. He kept his eyes on Lionel. "Was this part of your plan, sir?"

Lionel gave him an innocent look. "What do you mean?"

"Did you want the woman you brought here to get together with me after you've left us? What if I fall in love with her?"

Lionel smiled, and Donald felt a sweeping affection for the old man.

"I'll just say this, son. It will make a dying, very old man very happy to know that he has brought two loving people together. If that is what happens, I cannot be happier, and you have my blessing."

20

Aileen stared at the chair Lionel usually sat in. He had not come down to dinner. It frustrated her because she'd wanted to talk to him and tell him about their adventure with the bull the day before. He hadn't been there for dinner nor breakfast, and she never saw him at lunch, so she didn't expect him then.

Mary came from the other room, carrying the tray she always made for him.

"Wait, Mary," Aileen demanded, standing up abruptly. Mary almost dropped the tray, and Aileen apologized. "I didn't mean to scare you, please, if you will do me a favor. I want you to leave this here." She took the large tray and set it on an open spot on the table. Mary looked at her like she had two heads.

Aileen just smiled. "Go and fetch another tray and lid. I will walk with you to Lionel's room and have dinner with him there on his veranda. He is alone too much, and I don't like it."

The look of appreciation on Mary's face was not lost on Aileen. She was gone and back in only a few minutes, carrying a matching tray. Aileen helped her put Aileen's dinner plate, cup, and utensils on the tray, and Mary put the lid on it.

"I'll carry my tray," Aileen said. "You carry Lionel's."

"Yes, ma'am." Mary bent her knees and picked up Lionel's tray.

They walked together down the hall on the opposite side of the spiral staircase from the library and the office. Lionel only had to walk a short distance to get to his office, but it was on the other side of the house, which Aileen thought was a little strange for the frail old man. She assumed it would be good exercise for him when he needed it most.

Mary set her tray on the folding table next to the door so she could knock. As soon as she rapped her knuckles against the wooden door, she opened it, crouched to pick up the tray, and went in the room, singing Lionel's name cheerfully.

The old man was already out on the veranda.

Catching sight of the back of his head, Aileen felt a sharp twist in her heart. He didn't seem to be moving.

She hurried to follow Mary outside, turning quickly to look at Lionel. He had his eyes covered with a soft piece of fabric, and his head was tilted back.

"Sir?" Mary reached forward and jostled his shoulder gently.

Lionel snorted and sat forward suddenly, grabbing the eye cover from his face.

"Oh," he cried out. "Must have fallen asleep."

Relief swept through Aileen. She would have been devastated had anything happened to Lionel this soon after her arrival.

"You gave me a scare, Lionel," she stated firmly.

"I'm sorry, dear," Lionel responded, rubbing his eyes with his balled-up fists. "I didn't mean to do that. I'm afraid scares will be common with a man my age. Something we must expect, you know."

"I don't want to," Aileen teased.

Mary gave her an amused look, a bright smile on her face as she emptied the trays onto the table, setting their places for them.

When Mary was gone, Aileen pulled her chair closer to the table and gave the old man a pat on the hand. "Eat your food, Lionel McArthur, or I'll have to feed it to you, and we all know you don't want that."

"Oh no, I definitely don't." He chuckled, leaning forward to pick up his fork.

They were both quiet for ten minutes while they ate. Finally, it was Aileen who broke the silence.

"I noticed when I got here how loyal your people are to you, Lionel. You should be proud of that. I don't think you really needed me to come and take over. These people would have defended all this land if you'd left it to them."

"Well, we can't go back in time," the man responded, "and I'm so glad you are here now. You may be the strongest advocate I turn out to have."

Aileen shook her head. "No, sir. That distinction belongs to Donald. It's obvious he would protect you to his death."

She noticed the look of affection that came to his face. It made her heart happy.

"Donald is a fine young man. I have no doubt that he will protect my property to the best of his ability." He gave her a direct look, holding a biscuit in one hand. "And he will protect you, as well. I can already tell you two have a connection."

She grinned at him. "Are you playing matchmaker, Lionel? You bad boy."

He chuckled, throwing his head back a little. "I may have been doing just that, my dear. And I don't mind telling you why. Henry is a wonderful foreman. He knows everything about this business and this particular ranch."

Aileen thought of how the big man had started to chase down the bull. She might have stopped it, but Henry had fearlessly run after it and had probably brought the animal back to its pen on the other occasions it got out.

"But I knew when I saw Donald that I had an opportunity on my hands. He is a kind, loving, gentle soul. I think he's a bit shy. He's twenty-nine years old, and I've never seen him successfully snag a lady in the ten years he's been here. It's a waste. He will make a fine husband. If there is a match made between the two of you, you have my blessing. Besides, you will make children that look like my father. Who knows? Maybe someday in the future, my children's children's children will change their name and carry on my legacy without the blood relation."

"How ambitious of you," Aileen said with a smile.

"You don't really mind, do you?" Lionel asked. "I would hate to think I'm forcing something on you that you don't want."

Aileen shook her head emphatically. "Not at all. You have been nothing but kind and gracious to me since I got here."

"I don't have much choice, do I?" Lionel responded. "I need you, Aileen, desperately. I need you to keep my money and my estate out of the hands of those scummy stepsons of mine. You will do that for me, won't you?"

"I've told you before, and I will keep reassuring you, Lionel," Aileen said more firmly than ever, "I will not let them touch a single thing that was yours."

Lionel reached across the table and placed his hand flat on it. She covered his hand with hers and smiled.

"So you are pleased with being here, then?" he asked softly.

She nodded. "Yes. And your library is amazing. I can't wait to read all the ones I've never read before. The Winchesters had a grand library, and you have books they didn't have. That's very exciting to me."

"Ahh, the love of reading." Lionel sounded wistful. "I used to love to read. I can't anymore. It is a strain on my eyes, and I get a headache."

Aileen tilted her head to the side, compassion filling her. "I'm sorry, Lionel. Would you like me to read to you sometime? I don't mind. I love reading aloud and wouldn't mind doing that for you."

"I'd like that, Aileen." He turned his hand over, so hers was resting in his palm. "I'd like that very much."

21

A week had passed, and Aileen was missing her family in Shady Forks more than ever. She'd been writing to them and letting them know how happy she was. It wasn't the same, though, and after seeing Belle for more than a decade every single day, it was hard not missing her most of all.

She was having breakfast with Lionel on the veranda off of his room. It had become a daily ritual for Aileen to eat her meals with him. He was a funny character, cracking wise jokes and making her laugh all the time. She couldn't believe that a man that spirited was so sure he was going to die soon.

She left him that morning to take a ride through

the woods with Donald. He was waiting for her in the stables when she got there.

"Good morning," Donald said with a smile. "You ready to go for another adventure?"

She smiled back. "Every day is an adventure with you, Donald."

His eyebrows shot up. "Really? I didn't think I was that exciting."

She laughed as he helped her up into the saddle on her horse.

After some idle chit-chat and letting the horses meander at their own pace, Aileen asked him a question that had been on her mind since she'd arrived ten days ago.

"I've been wondering something," she began. "There's nothing in the house that indicates Lionel's stepsons were ever living there. I've been through all the rooms, and none of them are set up in case the men visit. In fact, they don't seem to have any property that I've noticed at all, not even a portrait hanging on a wall somewhere or any photographs."

Donald shook his head, keeping his eyes out in front of him. "There wouldn't be. Lionel doesn't want to even remember they are alive. I don't think he ever told them they were banned from the ranch, but I wouldn't be surprised if they assumed they were, and that's why they never come around. We're all glad they don't. We don't want them here. They get Lionel all excited. He doesn't need that in his condition."

"What is his condition?"

Donald turned his head to look at her, a blank expression on his face. "What?"

"What is his condition?" she repeated. "I've never asked. It doesn't seem to be too debilitating or painful. Is it just old age, and he thinks he's going to die because of that? Old age?"

Donald looked thoughtful. "I don't exactly know if he's got some illness or something. That's a question you'd have to ask Dr. St. Pierre. He'd answer whatever you asked him. He is very open about everything. That's one of the reasons Lionel likes him so much. Lionel likes the kind of people who will tell it like it is and not put sugar on top."

Aileen nodded. "I noticed that. Bertie seems to be just his type. I'm surprised they don't have anything going on."

Donald laughed. "Bertie? She's got to be—what —fifty-five at most? She's still too young for Lionel."

Aileen held her arms out to her sides and raised her eyebrows.

He shook his head. "Nu-uh. You don't count.

Totally different circumstance. He didn't fall in love with you. He sent for you. Not trying to offend you."

She pretended to be insulted for a second or two before laughing. "I know you're right. I'm just teasing."

They rode for another ten minutes, pointing out oddities and beautiful flower patches to each other as they went.

Aileen spotted something in a clearing beyond a patch of trees and slowed her horse. "Donald, wait. Do you see that?"

Donald stopped his horse and turned in the saddle to look at her. "What are you talking about?" he asked, swinging his gaze in the direction she was looking. "What do you see? What am I supposed to see... oh." He narrowed his eyes. "In that clearing over there?"

"Yeah," Aileen answered. She squinted and focused hard but couldn't tell what the blue object was.

"Well, let's go and see."

They left the trail behind and slowly made their way to the clearing. The closer they got, the more Aileen could smell the smoke from burning wood. She tried to peer around Donald, who was in front of her but couldn't really see anything until they both came out of the woods into the clearing.

"Would you look at that?" Donald said, wonder in his voice. He slid out of the saddle and left his horse to move to the ring of stones that had served as a firepit. The blue Aileen had seen was fabric thrown on top of the burning embers, which were still smoldering underneath.

"Is it poachers?" Aileen asked, turning to the left and the right in her saddle. Poachers were dangerous. They were only out to hunt animals.

"Probably." Donald's voice was annoyed. He picked up the fabric and shook it in the air, the burning parts lighting up when he did so. He dropped it on the ground and stomped on it until he was satisfied it wasn't on fire.

Aileen got down from her horse and looked around the makeshift campsite for any clues as to who might have been staying there. She didn't know anyone, but if she found anything, Donald might know who it belonged to. In either case, the sheriff should be notified.

Her thoughts were quiet as she stared at the ground, looking for clues. She wasn't really sure what she was looking for.

"Maybe one or two of the ranch hands stayed here for a night or something," she suggested quietly. "I can't see them leaving anything behind, if so. They'd only have to come back and get it at any time."

She watched Donald moving around the area, looking irritated.

"I don't think it was one of our guys. I'll tell you what I really think." He turned an angry face toward her. She didn't like it when he was angry, she decided. It didn't take away from his appeal, but she knew it wasn't a pleasant feeling. "I think it was those stepsons."

A chill ran over Aileen's skin. She had yet to see what the men looked like. She had them pictured in her head as disfigured monsters. "Oh no," she murmured. "What are you going to do?"

"I'll have to tell Lionel. See what he wants to do. This is his land. And I think he's got somebody watching the boys, so if they are here, they will be found out quick."

"Well, I don't want to be here anymore. It's things like this that make me miss Shady Forks and my family so much. I don't want to be in danger, for goodness sake."

Donald turned wide eyes to her. "You aren't backing out of the arrangement because of this, are you?"

Aileen shook her head but maintained a serious expression. "No, I can't leave Lionel now. Especially if those boys are here. They might hurt him."

"They can't change his will at this point," Donald added. "I hope they know that. They can't do anything about what's already been done legally."

"it's the illegal stuff I'm worried about. We don't have any idea what they've done."

Aileen hurried back to her horse and mounted, her heart aching for Shady Forks and the Winchester family. "I want to go back, Donald. Right now. Can we please go?"

Donald nodded, pulling up into his saddle and moving the horse, so he was next to her. "You go ahead and take the lead. You know the way back, don't you?"

"Yes." She urged the horse to go back toward the trail that would take them to the ranch. She was tired again and wanted a nap. Her fear of the stepsons was, at times, overwhelming.

Donald rode quietly behind her. She wondered what he was thinking. They parted at the house, though he came in with her and went down the hall to Lionel's office while she went up the stairs to rest in her room.

22

———

Lionel was seated behind the desk this time when Donald entered. The first thing to cross Donald's mind was that the old man looked tired. He usually looked tired, but today it was more prominent than usual.

"You feeling okay, boss?" he asked, going to the desk and standing in front of him, studying the man. Lionel stood up, and they shook hands.

"I'm all right for now, son." Lionel sat back down slowly. Concern filled Donald's chest, making his heart feel warm. "Sit, sit. To what do I owe the pleasure of this visit?"

"I want to do something for Aileen that I think she'll really like. I wanted to get your approval."

"What is it you had in mind?" The old man

looked intrigued. "And why do you need my permission?"

"Because I want to go to Shady Forks, where Aileen is from, to talk to her family there. The family she left behind. She's missing them so much. I was hoping they would come here and visit her. It would make her feel so much better. And if they'd like to stay for a little while, I know we have plenty of room. But of course, this is your house, and I need your permission to bring anyone here."

Lionel grinned from ear to ear, making Donald happy. "I think that's a wonderful idea, son. You don't want to take the stagecoach? I can give you the money for the ride if you need it." Lionel moved like he was going to pull out his money.

Donald lifted one hand and waved it dismissively in the air. "No, no. I don't need your money, sir. You have always been more than generous with us. I would rather take my own horse and just ride out there. It will only take me a few hours if I push my horse only a little. I won't stop anywhere. It wouldn't be a problem for me at all. And I know how much it would mean to Aileen."

He felt the weight of Lionel's eyes on his face. He wondered what the old man was thinking. He didn't have to wait long to find out. As per usual, Lionel went ahead and told him.

"You are falling for her aren't you, Donald?"

Donald felt his face turn warm. He looked down at his hands. There was no way around it. He was in love with his boss's wife. And the best thing about it was it had been arranged by Lionel himself.

"I believe so, yes," he answered without lifting his eyes.

"You have no need to be ashamed, young man," Lionel responded. Donald had to look up because of the tone in the old man's voice. He sounded utterly delighted. The smile on his face confirmed how he was feeling. "I am overjoyed that you feel for her that way. I know she has similar feelings for you."

Donald's chest tingled with excitement. "Does she? You're sure?"

"You must know by now, son. If you don't, you are blind as a bat and deaf as a stone."

Donald laughed. "Is it that obvious to you?"

"I have many more years of experience than you do, Donald. Trust me. She is yours if you want her. But you must be kind and gentle with her. You will be, won't you?"

"Yes, I definitely will."

"You will treat her with the respect she deserves?"

Donald nodded. An overwhelming sadness came over him as he gazed into the old man's eyes. He resisted the urge to ask if he could hug him. "Yes, sir," he stated firmly.

"I think you and she will take good care of each other when I'm gone. Two strong people like you will be able to fight off those two dirty dogs, and you'll have Henry as a third person to provide even more strength. I'm counting on the three of you. You know that."

"Yes, Lionel. I wish you would stop worrying so much. You need to spend your days in happiness, enjoying whatever it is that makes you happy, instead of worrying about what will happen when you aren't here. We will take care of everything. I promise you. I swear it on the graves of my parents. We will protect what's yours and continue to grow it."

Lionel's eyes were moist, and the old man blinked rapidly, pressing the side of his finger in his eye to catch the tears that threatened to fall.

Donald was about to leave the office when he remembered he'd made plans to eat dinner with Aileen and Lionel.

"Oh," he said, turning back to Lionel. "Dinner. I was supposed to eat with the two of you tonight."

Lionel shook his head, waving his hand. "Don't you worry, son. I'll explain it to Aileen."

"You're not going to tell her where I've gone, are you?" he asked, surprised that the old man would even think about ruining the surprise like that.

Lionel chuckled, giving Donald a sarcastic look. "No, young man. I'm going to tell her that I've sent you off on business and that you will likely return in the middle of the night or even tomorrow. If they offer to keep you for the night, you go ahead and do that. At this rate, you will get there at dinnertime, and if you left within the hour, you wouldn't be here till the wee hours. Best to just stay if you are invited. From the way she talks about them, I believe all you'll have to do is ask. They sound like a very friendly bunch of people."

Donald agreed with Lionel's assessment of the Winchester family in Shady Forks.

"Thank you, Lionel. I'm glad you approve of this."

"I'll have the girls make up several rooms for them. I do believe they have children. The nursery here hasn't been opened in years. I wonder if there are still toys in it. If so, they are about a hundred years old."

"So rocks and sticks then?"

Both men laughed, and Donald left, a big smile on his face. He was pleased Lionel had agreed to his idea. He went directly out the door, glancing over his shoulder up the stairs. He didn't want Aileen to see him. His horse was waiting out front, just where he'd left it. Aileen's was there, too, but he led the animal to the stables and called Jonah to come out and get him.

After leaving Aileen's horse with the groom, Donald got up in the saddle and headed for Gustaf's Corner. He would need to get a map so he could find his way. Hopefully, they had some extras at the stagecoach station.

He managed to get out of there without anyone seeing him other than Jonah, who he didn't tell where he was going. There was no need to tell him that.

He got his horse moving at a good steady pace, not galloping but not trotting either. The terrain was smooth the entire way, as far as he knew. He would be sticking to the roads, and generally, a horse could traverse that land a lot smoother than a wagon or a buggy.

Once Donald was out of Gustaf's Corner, he set the horse to a faster pace. He leaned forward and gave all his energy to the horse. He didn't want to wear it out, but he had to get to Shady Forks as fast as possible. Nonstop at a fast pace would get him there around dinnertime, just as Lionel had said. He wanted to get there before dark. It would be worse for him to try to see in the darkness while traveling along black roads than it would be to interrupt them at their dinner table.

Besides, he had left in such a hurry, he hadn't brought along anything to eat.

He was going to be starving to death by the time he got there.

23

Once Donald reached Shady Forks, he had to stop at the saloon to ask where the Winchester ranch could be found. The bartender was more than obliging, taking out a piece of paper and scrawling directions on it with a pen.

He thanked the man and headed toward the ranch, his directions out. The sun was about to set, and he wanted to hurry up and get there.

Finally, he turned onto the long driveway of the Winchester ranch. It didn't look like the one in Gustaf's Corner. The McArthur ranch was much more lavish. It was no wonder Aileen had reacted the way she did. The Winchester ranch was rich with beauty, but it was like a child's garden next to the castle-like appearance of the McArthur house.

Not that the fact made Donald think any less of the Winchesters. According to Aileen, they were the wealthiest in the town and just chose to be humble about it.

He dismounted in front of the porch steps and went quickly up to the wooden porch, taking two at a time. He knocked on the door, trying not to feel as anxious as he really was.

The door was opened by a petite young woman with dark hair. She had a friendly look on her face. It took a moment, but Donald realized she had to be a maid or something like that.

"I'm looking for Theresa? Winchester? Or... Nate, I think?"

The girl nodded. "Come in and wait, please. I'll tell them. And whom shall I say is here?"

Donald thought about it for a second. "Tell them Lionel McArthur."

He didn't say that he was Lionel. Just that he was there. He wasn't, technically, but he was sent by him. That had to make a difference, didn't it?

The girl disappeared and then reappeared, a big smile on her face. "They said to come through. They are having dinner and hope you won't be disrespected if they continue to eat while you have your conversation."

Donald nodded. "I'm fine with that."

He followed her into the large dining room that looked similar to the one at the ranch back home in Gustaf's Corner. There were four adults at the table and a smattering of children mixed in between. The children were eating quietly, and when he came into the room, all motion stopped so they could look at him.

"Mr. McArthur." One of the men got up and came over, his hand extended. "It's so good to meet you. We've heard a lot about you from Aileen's letters. You're a lot younger than I expected, though."

Donald blushed to his roots. He hadn't even thought about the fact that Aileen would have written to her family and told them what was going on. He'd expected her to keep the true facts from them since things worked out well in the end. But then, how could she explain being with a man who had a different name than that of the man she married?

"Donald Ferris, actually," he said, pumping the man's hand.

To his credit, the man never lost his smile. "Nate Winchester." He turned to the others. "This is

Theresa, my wife. There's my brother, Rich, and his wife, Annie." The other members of the family waved and smiled at him. "Those are all the kids, and even if I told you all their names, you probably wouldn't remember them. Doubtful you'll be spending a lot of time with them."

"Is Aileen okay?" Theresa asked, sounding like she was waiting for her husband to simply take a breath so she could ask the question. "If you don't mind me saying so, sir, you look haggard, as if you tried to get here as fast as you could.

"I did," he responded, "but not because there's something wrong with Aileen. There's no emergency. The only real emergency is how much she misses you. It's a tragedy, really. And you all being so close, I thought, I should go down there and get them for a surprise visit." He grinned wide. "I can't really fit all of you on the back of my horse, so I reckon I'm not really getting you. But I am asking. If you can spare a little time for Aileen. She misses you and needs to see you." He swept his eyes over the adults. "She needs to see all of you. But mostly you, Theresa. She talks about you all the time. I know her heart is aching. It's been ten days after ten years, and she is suffering."

"You rode nonstop to come and tell us that she

misses us?" Theresa asked breathlessly, her eyes wide.

He nodded.

She turned her gaze to Annie and then Nate. "Did you hear that?" She stood up and came around the table, holding her arms out. To Donald's surprise, she pulled him into a tight hug. The other adults surrounded him, patting him on the back. They returned to their seats, but Theresa stayed in front of him, holding his cheeks in her hands.

"You are a good man. I'm so glad she found a good man. She told us in her letters how it all started, and frankly, we were a little afraid for her. But that didn't last long, did it. We hardly had time to contemplate coming to rescue her when she went on in that very same letter to tell us how it all turned out. She was mighty surprised, but this Lionel McArthur sounds like a gentleman through and through."

Donald nodded. "He didn't used to be, so he claims. So he's making up for lost time now by being extra good to people. I just happen to be one of the lucky ones."

"And Aileen is, too, I guess. Come on over and sit down. We can always clear an extra chair. Noah, you're done eating, right? Go ahead and give the man your chair."

The young boy in the chair next to Rich Winchester got up obligingly, picking up his plate with him. "I can go sit next to Adam." He smiled at Donald to let him know there were no hard feelings and went to the end of the table, where there was an empty chair next to another little boy. The two smiled at each other when Noah sat down.

"Are you hungry?" Theresa asked. "You're welcome to have dinner with us."

"I would very much like that. Tell me, though, what would you all say if I invited you back to the ranch in Gustaf's Corner to have an extended visit with Aileen? I know she would like that so very much."

Theresa looked delighted, but she turned her eyes to her husband for the answer. Nate smiled at his wife. "Of course we can go there for a visit. Gustaf's Corner isn't far from here. We can come back to take care of work, can't we, Rich?"

"I don't see why not. We do have a foreman for when we aren't around, don't we? I think we can leave the ranch in his capable hands for a week or so."

Donald was amused to see Theresa bouncing in

her seat. He expected her to come out of her skin in a moment. Or at least off the chair. "Oh, that's wonderful," she cried, clapping her hands together. "That's just wonderful." She leaned forward and looked down toward the children. "Did you hear that? We're going on a vacation."

Donald couldn't resist the urge to talk up Lionel's castle home. "And wait till you see it. It's amazing. Beautiful. Your land here is quite beautiful, as well. But wait till you see what my boss has done. He's spared no expense, I can tell you that."

"It sounds wonderful, Donald," Annie said. "Thank you for thinking of us and coming to ask us. It was very nice of you. You could have just written to us."

"I think Aileen is overdue for a visit from her family," he said. "Ten days is a long time for her to be without you all."

24

Aileen stood on the porch, her arms crossed over her chest, a frown on her slender face. She was annoyed with both Lionel and Donald. Lionel told her at dinner last night—a dinner where she'd been looking forward to seeing Donald at—that he'd sent the second foreman off on some impromptu business trip that no one else could possibly go on.

Her irritated thoughts were only interrupted by brief moments of humor where she'd stick out her bottom lip and feel like stomping her foot. She wouldn't throw a tantrum, she told herself. She was thirty years old. What would that look like?

She brooded a little longer, staring out at the empty driveway in front of her, trying to wish him into coming back. It would be a boring day without him, she grumbled to herself.

Finally, just when she was about to go inside and get a snack and a book to read, she saw dust kicked up at the end of the road. Her heartbeat sped up, and she leaned forward as if those few inches would let her see if it was Donald or not. It had to be him, she thought. Who else could it be? No one ever visited the McArthur Ranch except the usuals, and they rarely came early in the day. Lionel liked to reserve any business meetings for the afternoon because he claimed he didn't function until the sun was high above his head and the clock was striking noon.

Aileen had heard the ranch hands tease about that, saying it must be nice to be leisurely until midday. She didn't have to defend Lionel. The ranch hands meant no disrespect.

It only took a few moments for her to see that it was, in fact, the man she was waiting for. She squealed softly and clapped her hands together, hopping up and down. She grabbed her skirt and was about to jump down the steps when she stopped short, seeing a buggy pulling in behind Donald's horse. It was one of those long family buggies. She hadn't seen one here in Gustaf's Corner in the time she'd been there. The one coming toward the ranch looked awfully familiar. It looked just like—

Tears immediately clogged Aileen's throat and filled her eyes. She clapped one hand over her mouth after sucking in a breath to try to hold the tears in.

It was the Winchester family. Children were hanging out the sides in the back, and when they saw her, they started to scream her name.

She started to laugh and ran down the stairs being extra careful till she hit the ground and then went full tilt toward the oncoming horse and buggy. Donald stopped before she got to him and the buggy pulled up beside him. Aileen ran to Donald first to swat at him and then throw her arms around him.

"Oh, what have you done?" she cried, happy tears streaming down her face. "What have you done?"

"I fetched your family for you," Donald responded in a proud voice.

"You did. You did." Aileen laughed as she spoke, hugging him one more time before leaving him behind to grab hold of Theresa.

They were all talking at once as the men helped the children out of the buggy, and the ladies talked as if they hadn't seen each other for a year. Aileen wasn't surprised that the women gushed about the beauty of McArthur Ranch. The little ones surrounded her, holding onto her legs and trying to get her attention. She made sure to give all of them a hug and a kiss on the cheek. It wasn't until she saw them all that she realized how much her heart had truly missed them.

She took the ladies inside, leaving Donald outside with the men and children. She wanted them to meet Lionel as soon as they got there.

"Donald has asked us to stay for an extended visit, and Nate said that's all right. You don't mind, do you?"

Aileen laughed. "Of course not. I guess he got permission from Lionel. I'm sure Lionel wouldn't have minded even if he didn't." She gestured with her hands, her excitement getting away from her. She hurried down the hall. "Come on. I want you to meet him. You're going to love him, I promise."

She tapped on the door to his office and went in when he said to. He looked up from his desk and smiled at her. "Good morning, afternoon, dear." His eyes moved to the other ladies as they came in behind Aileen. He sat back, his smile widening. "And who do we have here? The Winchester ladies?"

"Yes," Aileen said enthusiastically. "Thank you

for letting them visit, Lionel. I wanted them to meet you right away."

The ladies went to him and shook hands. They each chatted briefly with him, mostly with Annie and Theresa flooding him with compliments about the castle-styled ranch with the unique windows and the incredible lawn and driveway.

"You must show them around the house and the grounds, my dear," Lionel said to Aileen. She nodded, clapping her hands together lightly.

"Oh yes. I will show them my room first. You have to see this to believe it."

She hurried up the steps, talking excitedly to Theresa and Annie.

"I've never been treated like this before in my life. I mean it. You girls just won't believe it. All of this will be mine. And don't get me wrong, I don't want Lionel going anywhere."

"You've grown quite fond of him, haven't you?" Theresa asked, her smile beaming from her face.

"I have," Aileen spoke in a soft voice. She got a warm feeling in her heart when she thought about Lionel. He was so much more than a benefactor, which was what he would have been under any other circumstances. He had taken a poor girl and given her everything. Not supplied her with her needs or paid her a good wage like the Winchesters. He was *giving* everything to her. His death would make her an instant millionairess.

Aileen didn't think about it in those terms, though. The thoughts never crossed her mind. There was every chance Lionel could live for another ten, fifteen, or even twenty years, not that a hundred was a viable goal to shoot for.

The ladies oohed and aahed her bedroom, moving to the closet to admire some more and then the washroom with the large tub and the running water.

"This is amazing, Aileen. He really did so much for you, didn't he? He's making this your home."

"He sure is."

Theresa dropped down to sit on the edge of the bed while Annie took the chair by the window.

"And you have love in your life, too. I can't tell you how surprised we all were to hear that Lionel McArthur was at the door."

Aileen raised her eyebrows. "He said he was Lionel? Why would he do that?"

"I reckon he thought we wouldn't know who he was. That you hadn't written to us about him."

"And if you did write," Annie added, "there was no way for him to know what you said about him.

Because of what he did, going along with the marriage ceremony and all."

"I forgave him for that the first day," Aileen said.

Theresa laughed. "Men can be clueless sometimes. Either way, when we saw him, we knew who he was. And it didn't bother us that he gave Lionel's name instead of his own. He's a nice man. I approve of him for you."

Aileen bit her bottom lip. She allowed herself to swoon in front of her friends, pressing her hands over her heart. "I think he is the man I will truly marry. I have never felt about anyone the way I feel about him."

"Is it love then?" Theresa asked, her face radiating happiness.

Aileen nodded. "I really do think so. I can't see it being anything else."

Both Theresa and Annie jumped up at the same time and ran toward Aileen. She was surprised at first and then started laughing as her friends wrapped her in a group hug. They jumped up and down with her. Aileen hadn't done that since she was a little girl.

She'd forgotten how fun it was.

<h1 style="text-align:center">25</h1>

It had been one of the best days of Aileen's life. Lionel had come down for dinner with everyone and turned out to be the life of the party, telling funny stories from his youth and some harrowing adventures as well that kept the children enraptured so that when it was time for them to go to bed, they didn't want to go.

They had played cards until late in the evening and had plans to stay up even longer. She was looking forward to getting revenge for having been beaten repeatedly at Spades. She'd warned Donald she was going to get another partner if he didn't learn the game. He'd just laughed at her, and she knew why. It wasn't Donald that didn't know how to play the game well.

She laughed at herself as she stood there, remembering how much fun she'd had. How much fun they'd all had. Laughing and playing down by the creek, the children splashing and swimming, screaming like they were being killed when they were only having fun.

Aileen had missed those moments. She wanted the Winchester families to stay until she got married and had her own children. Then they could leave, and she wouldn't feel quite so alone. There weren't any children on the McArthur Ranch, and that felt so strange to her.

Lionel had retired early, which Aileen completely understood. He had done the best he could, but he truly was looking frailer than ever. It frightened Aileen, but she wouldn't let it be known, at least not to him. He said he was on his way out, but it was obvious he didn't want to leave his mortal body for his heavenly one.

She stared out into the night sky, wondering if she would ever be that old. If she lived that long, would she be ready to go? Or would she want to hold on, even though eighty years had passed?

The ladies were inside putting their children in the beds Theresa and Mary had made up for them, and the men were in the parlor with Donald and

Henry. She was outside, getting a bit of fresh air and enjoying the moonlight. The men would likely join her at some point.

She rubbed her arms up and down when a stiff breeze blew over her. She walked to the edge of the deck and looked out toward the front yard, scanning what she could see in the darkness. A million stars twinkled above her, and the moon was full, casting almost as much light down as the sun did during the day. Except it bathed the earth with white, a comforting, mellow light that made Aileen feel like heaven had come down for a while.

She swept her eyes over the land. Someday this would all be hers. She would own everything she saw and had done absolutely nothing to get it. How she could be so blessed was beyond her comprehension.

And, as Theresa said, to find love at the same time. It seemed like a miracle. Her life had completely changed in such a short time. She was on top of the world. Happier than she'd ever been before.

She turned to look over her shoulder when she heard the men burst out in laughter. For a second, she thought they were going to come through the door at any moment. But after the laughter died down, she heard nothing, which meant they were still in the parlor.

She turned back and looked at the lawn again, staring out at the sculptures, the trimmed bushes, the flowers that looked black, white, and grey in the moonlight.

A twinkle within the trees caught her eye, and she focused on it. She couldn't think of anything down that way that would look like that. There was nothing that could flash out there, and what would it be reflecting? The lamps hanging from the front porch didn't give off nearly enough light for that. She could see shadows in the distance and the shapes of the trees and other objects. But there was nothing that should be giving off or reflecting light where she was looking.

She leaned forward and then walked to the railing to bend over it, holding onto the edges.

Aileen blinked several times and leaned further out until she almost lost her balance. She felt a little dizzy and pulled back just in time before she pitched forward. Looking over her shoulder at the house, she pondered whether she should go see what it was or bother the men with it. It looked to her like a lantern. A lit lantern sitting on the shore of the creek. They had all been playing down there until dinnertime, including the children. Mostly the children, really, as the adults walked around talking about the incredible landscaping of McArthur Ranch.

What if one of them left a lantern burning? That seemed like something a child would do.

She remembered the campsite she and Donald had stumbled on. But that wasn't near there. That was much further up along the creek line. Whoever it was had likely cleared out by now. Donald hadn't mentioned it since.

She didn't want to look silly in front of her family. Nor did she want to scare Theresa and Annie with the idea that there might be something to be afraid of at McArthur Ranch. The only thing she hadn't mentioned to them was the two evil brothers and the threat they posed to the ranch and to her. She was sure she could handle them in court. Mark Handelburg had a good reputation, according to Lionel, and she didn't have a thing to worry about.

She chose to believe Lionel. He had a lot more experience in life than she did. Surely he could tell about people at his age. She doubted anyone could hide anything from that brilliant curmudgeon.

She decided to quickly check the creek to see if that was what she was actually seeing. Glancing back at the house once more, she hurried across the lawn. She had to go almost all the way to the woods between the property and the main road on the other side.

As Aileen got closer, she could see that it was indeed a lit lantern. It was set at about a medium beam and was facing toward the house.

"Those silly children," she murmured. She headed for the lantern and reached out for it, taking the metal handle in her hand.

The next moment, everything went dark. She felt something abruptly stuffed into her mouth. It stank badly. A burlap sack had been pulled over her head. She could tell because she let go of the lantern and reached up to try to pull it off.

"What? What's this? Stop. What are you doing?" Aileen felt the commotion around her as the burlap sack was pulled tight, and something went around her neck to secure it. Her arms were pulled behind her. In those few seconds, though, she had started to run and kick, flailing about like a madwoman, trying her best to get away, even though she couldn't see. She would likely run straight into a tree, but she didn't care.

Something that felt like a rope was wrapped

around her wrists. Then her ankles. She lost her balance but continued to wriggle.

Fear sliced into her painfully. She felt herself being lifted up as if she was weightless. Her stomach slammed into something that could only be a shoulder. She continued to struggle, trying to spit out the gag with no success, her tongue rendered useless under the thick, stinky fabric.

She moved and squirmed until she had no energy left. Her stomach hurt terribly from bouncing on the shoulder of what was probably a very burly man. She let herself break down into tears until it was quiet and dark, and she moved into unconsciousness.

26

Aileen came to the moment the bag was pulled from her head. She shook it as hard as she could, struggling to spit out the cloth in her mouth. When it became slightly dislodged, she pressed her tongue against it, much to her disgust, and lobbed it from her mouth.

"How dare you," she shrieked at the top of her lungs. "What do you think you're doing?"

She glared at the two men in front of her. Both were sneering at her, their faces so similar, she instantly knew who they were. They had to be Conrad and Buster. Who else would have had the nerve to take her and tie her up in a cabin?

She looked all around her but didn't recognize anything. She'd heard of a hunting cabin Lionel and his father had used, but she'd never been to it. The darkness she saw through the window of the cabin told her it was still nighttime. She didn't feel like a long time had passed and chose to believe she had only passed out from shock for a moment. She felt no pain other than her stomach and knew they hadn't assaulted her in any way.

But they looked like they wanted to. The daggers they sent with their eyes sent a shiver down Aileen's spine. She wouldn't back down, though.

"What do you want from me?" she demanded. "I can't do anything for you."

"You are going to stay here tonight," one of them said. He looked slightly younger, so she was going to assume he was Conrad.

"Conrad here is gonna go get the old man. He's gonna sign a new will right here in front of us. We heard what he did, and we won't let him get away with it."

Aileen was furious. She pulled her eyebrows together and surged forward even though her hands were still tied behind her back and her feet were together underneath her. "What are you talking about? He hasn't done anything to you."

"He cut us out of his will."

Aileen laughed without humor. "I heard he did

that a long time ago, boys. You aren't going to get anywhere with this. And what if he dies while you're kidnapping him, huh? What if you bring him here and then end up shooting him? Do you really think I'm going to let you get away with that? I'll tell everyone."

"Then we will kill you," Conrad yelled at her, coming close to her face. She smelled stale tobacco and cringed, pulling away from him.

"And everyone will know you did it," Aileen raged. "They will know. The ranch hands know who you are, the staff in the house know who you are. They will all testify that it had to be the two of you. You won't get away with this."

"If we don't get our way and the old man dies..." It was the other one who spoke, approaching her, and grabbed her by the chin, so his fingers pressed painfully into her cheeks, "you will be the one to suffer. We will torture you for the rest of your days. You will never be rid of us. And there won't be a thing you can do about it." He came close enough to her face to kiss her. Terror paralyzed her momentarily.

He didn't kiss her. Instead, he shoved her face to the side. She lost her balance and fell over. The floor of the cabin was dirty and cluttered with dust and debris from not being cleaned or used for many years. A dust cloud caught her in the face, and she breathed it in.

She immediately choked, flipping onto her back to cough. She used the momentum of the coughing to lift her up to a sitting position, where she continued to cough until she could breathe again.

Tears streamed from her eyes, and she lifted her shoulders alternately to wipe at them.

"I think she might die, and then we'll just get the money anyway. Won't even have to kill her."

She heard the remark and the laughter of both men and ignored it.

"You gotta go get the old man," Conrad said. "Bring him here. I got the documents all drawn up. He only has to sign it. Then we'll return him to the house, and they'll both live as long as they keep their mouths shut."

"What's to stop us from telling everyone what you've done to us tonight and that the document was signed under duress?" Aileen asked hotly.

Both men stared at her as if they didn't expect her to speak, much less ask a pertinent question. She curled her lip at them in disgust. She'd never seen two more vile human beings in her life.

"Because, lady," Buster growled, pulling a ten-inch blade from the sheath attached to his belt and holding it up under her nose, where he twisted it from side to side. "If you do say anything, I'll make sure that pretty face of yours ain't so pretty anymore."

"Don't say ain't, Buster," Conrad stated. "It's not classy. Remember what mum always said."

Buster glanced back at Conrad. "You're right. Sorry."

Aileen watched the two of them, her anger growing by the second. When Buster turned his head away from her, all she wanted to do was grab the knife. But her hands were still secured behind her back, and she had nothing to grab the knife with.

Buster turned back to her. "I'll make sure that pretty face of yours *isn't* so pretty anymore." He glanced back at Conrad who nodded, a satisfied look on his face.

Buster's smile when he turned once again to Aileen disgusted her. She wanted to spit on him, but he was holding that knife inches from her face, and it wouldn't take anything for him to just stick it in her somewhere. He might put her eye out with it. She wouldn't doubt it.

If given a chance, Aileen had no doubt these

men would kill her. Their reputation had done much to tarnish her impression of them but seeing them and hearing them right there in person solidified everything she'd heard about them.

The thought that it would be easier just to give them money than to put up with their violent selfishness flittered through her mind like a moth around a flame.

She extinguished the idea as quickly as it came. Giving them even one penny of Lionel's money would be an act of ultimate betrayal and disloyalty. He had stated time and again he didn't want them to have anything of his. No land, no property, no money.

Aileen remembered. She would not forget.

She kept quiet until Buster moved away, sliding the knife back in the sheath.

"Glad you know when to shut your mouth," he said, stepped away from her but keeping his eyes on her.

"You need to go get the old man before he gets too far into his sleep," Conrad said. "He has to be swift enough to sign his name and to understand not to say anything to anyone."

"Yeah, yeah." Buster headed for the front door. He turned when he got there and let out a small laugh. "Hey, we can just tell him this is all a dream, and he'll die thinking he never signed the new will."

They both laughed at that, and Buster went out, slamming the door behind him.

It seemed neither were concerned about the level of noise they were making. Aileen wondered if they knew she had visitors. That the Winchester brothers were not to be trifled with, and they cared deeply for her.

She could only pray that somehow the men would catch on to what was going on. They wouldn't allow Lionel to be taken. Normally, it would just be the two of them in the house. Just her and Lionel, safe in their beds. The servants in theirs or gone home. The ranch hands in the bunkhouse or their personal homes.

But tonight, the house was full.

And it was full of people who would go far out of their way to see that Aileen got home safe and sound.

Aileen lifted her chin, forcing herself to feel confident.

Everyone in that house loved her. They would come for her. She wasn't a fifth wheel anymore.

27

Donald poured two glasses of brandy and took them out on the porch to share with Aileen. He was sure he'd seen her come out there. She hadn't gone back inside. He was sure of it.

But when he stepped out on the empty porch, he doubted his own memory. Maybe she'd slipped past him. But why would she do that? Surely she wouldn't have gone to bed without telling him goodnight.

He set the glasses down on the porch table.

"Aileen?" he called out. He had no idea where she would have gone if she wasn't there. The front lawn was empty from what he could see. It was dark, so if she was hiding out there somewhere, he probably wouldn't be able to see her unless she moved.

Was she playing a game?

"Aileen?" he called louder.

If so, it wasn't funny.

He walked to the end of the deck on the right side and looked around the house. The trees cast long shadows across the ground, casting a thick black blanket over everything in its path.

Donald turned and went to the other side. It was easier to see on that side because there were fewer trees, and the moon was shining bright.

Donald didn't need moonlight to see the bobbing lantern in the distance, though. The light was coming from the back of the house and heading toward the creek. He pulled in his breath and was about to call out Aileen's name when the figure moved under the moon, and both men were bathed in its light.

Donald froze. He would know Buster anywhere. Even in the dark of night. His heart jumped into his throat when he realized it was Lionel he had with him and that the man was slumped over, a large blanket over his shoulders, no hat, and slippers on his feet that slapped against the ground as he was hurried along.

Aileen.

In his experience and from what he'd heard from others, Donald was aware that Conrad and Buster were dangerous, violent men. They would stop at nothing to get what they wanted, and that certainly pertained to money, if not anything else.

They had snatched Aileen from the porch, and now they had Lionel.

Fear gripped Donald. He watched Buster leading Lionel toward the creek, going back in his memory to search his internal map of the land.

He snapped his fingers as he ran back into the house to get the other men. "The hunting cabin," he told himself.

Henry was still there, discussing the finer things in life with the Winchester brothers when Donald burst into the parlor.

"The evil brothers are here," he said bluntly, his eyes on Henry.

Henry jumped to his feet. "What? Where?"

"Aileen isn't on the porch. I went around the side and saw Buster leading Lionel out to the creek."

"What's going on?" Rich asked, his voice booming through the room. Donald recognized the situation had caught the brothers off guard, and it angered them. "Is Aileen in trouble? Why weren't we told there was danger?"

Henry lifted his hands to pat the air down around him. "We need to stay calm. It's likely Conrad and Buster just want Lionel to sign a new will."

Rich grunted, sneering. "Children."

Donald looked at the tall man. "Stepchildren. Stepsons. And they are downright evil. That's why we call them the evil brothers. They're just plain awful. And I think they took Aileen and Lionel to that hunting cabin. I need your help. Will you come along?"

He was asking the Winchester brothers, and both of them nodded vigorously, moving toward the parlor door.

"Let's go."

"I don't think it would be wise to tell the ladies," Henry said as the four men headed toward the entrance. "They are fine with the children. The brothers don't want them. They want Lionel and Aileen."

"Lead us to the hunting cabin," Nate said. "We don't want Aileen getting hurt."

Donald felt bad about the situation. The thought ran through his mind that these fellows who deeply cared for Aileen might try to get her to go back with them. His heart quaked at the thought. He wanted her to stay with him for the rest of their lives. He would give anything to have her back in his arms for good.

He tried not to think any negative thoughts as he led the men out, down the porch steps, and toward the creek. He'd grabbed a lantern from the porch, unhooking it as he went down to the ground.

"How far away is this place?" Nate asked, coming up beside Donald as they made their way silently across the lawn. Donald could still see the lantern from Buster bobbing in the distance. He was heading straight for the cabin. They could lose him, and they'd still know where to go.

Donald wasn't impressed with the two brothers. They didn't seem to have much sense at all. They had never been smart, but to do this so openly was almost astounding.

He remembered that they probably had no idea there were so many people in the house. He silently thanked God they had chosen that particular night to pull their stunt.

Knowing how violent they could be, Donald's concern for both Lionel and Aileen grew. His chest was tight with anxiety long before he saw the cabin in the distance. When he did see it, it felt like he couldn't breathe for a moment. He had to take a second to compose himself, keeping his face turned away from the others, not that they could see much in the dark.

The light was shining through the windows of the cabin, indicating Buster and Lionel had reached their destination. There was no yelling or screaming. Donald didn't hear fighting of any kind, physically or verbally. The absence of screams from Aileen was a good sign.

Or it could be a bad one.

Donald refused to think that.

"Watch the light," Nate hissed, putting his hand out and resting it on Donald's hand that was holding the lantern, pushing it down.

Donald turned it to face away from the building, and they carefully made their way across the uneven terrain to the small cabin. He hadn't seen it in years. There was only one room inside, though it was fairly large, as hunting cabins went. The good thing about that was that there was nowhere for the brothers to hide their victims. Donald, Henry, and the brothers would be able to burst in and catch them by surprise.

Probably.

Donald pulled in a shaky breath, looking down.

"We have to cross the creek first?" Nate said under his breath, sounding bewildered.

"There's a swinging rope bridge up ahead," Donald whispered, tapping Nate on the shoulder and gesturing in the direction of the bridge. "But if we cross there, there's a good chance we'll be seen from inside if we use the light. But if we don't use the light, we can't see to cross the bridge."

Nate nodded, his eyes on the water running swiftly in front of them.

"Is it deep here? Maybe we can cross through the water. What about the current? Is it strong?"

"I don't really know. I've never tried." Donald stared at the darkness of the water. "I don't know if I want to risk a broken leg or neck to cross it on foot. We should take our chances with the bridge. I bet they're distracted in there, don't you think? Looking at Lionel and Aileen instead of the windows or door?"

Nate looked contemplative. He gestured to his brother and Henry, who came closer. The men huddled in a circle.

"We're going to the bridge. We'll cut the light down as low as we can. Take it real slow. We gotta trust that we got here soon enough, and those boys won't feel like killing for another twenty minutes at least."

Donald's heart shook at Nate's words. He nodded, ready to put his life on the line for the woman he loved.

28

Aileen was irate when Buster brought Lionel in and shoved him toward her. The old man stumbled and fell nearby on several old cushions lying on the floor. She was grateful they had broken his fall.

"Let my arms loose," she demanded. "I have to help him. Can't you see what you're doing to him?"

Conrad stared at Lionel, who was on his side, his eyes closed, not looking at them. He jerked his head at Aileen. "Untie her," he told Buster.

"But she—"

"I said untie her," Conrad yelled, making Buster jump.

Aileen turned her back and held her arms up as high as she could. Buster pulled the knife from his sheath, and she closed her eyes when he went around behind her back. She could almost feel the knife piercing her back. Instead, her arms were freed, and she immediately scooted over to where Lionel was, not worried about her feet. She could untie those after she made sure Lionel was alive.

"You worry too much about that old man," Conrad said in a softer voice than he'd been using before.

Aileen felt a measure of hope. If the two men could stop feeling so much hate, there was a good chance everyone would get out of this alive.

"Lionel," Aileen said, grabbing him by his thin shoulders and pulling him to her. "Lionel, are you alive? Are you all right?"

Lionel opened one eye and looked up at her. "I'm not gone yet," he whispered.

Relief flooded her body. "Oh, thank You, God. Thank You." She glanced up.

"Glad to see you're still alive, old man." Buster's voice boomed through the small cabin. "You got papers to sign. If you were already dead, your wife there would have endured years of hardship and pain because of you. Now you're gonna sign our papers and your new will makes us very, very rich. Doesn't it, brother?"

Conrad grinned at Buster. "It sure does, brother."

"I'll never sign anything over to the two of you," Lionel said, his voice hushed but still strong and extremely angry.

"Oh, yes you will." Buster stepped closer, putting his sharp blade very close to the old man's face. "If you know what's good for you. Because it won't be you we cut up. It will be her." He flipped the blade to Aileen and brought it close enough to her cheek that she felt it pierce her like a small insect bite. She backed away and put her hand up to her face. When she pulled it away, she saw a speck of blood there.

"You leave her alone," Lionel said in a louder voice, lifting up to a sitting position.

Aileen could see it took a lot of effort for him to do that. She hadn't realized how weak he was really getting.

"Stay calm, Lionel," she said in a warm voice, putting her hands on his upper arms to help him steady himself.

"Look at that. She's his caretaker. Some wife."

Both men laughed.

Aileen narrowed her eyes at them.

A flicker of light outside made her eyes flick to the side. She realized what she saw in an instant and moved her eyes back to the two men hoping they hadn't seen her look out there. She didn't want to draw their attention to it.

But what she'd seen filled her with elation. There was someone coming across the bridge. She'd seen it through the window when Buster crossed to go fetch Lionel. Now there was someone on it again. They were coming to get her.

"You should get out the papers you need him to sign and just get this over with," she said abruptly. She wanted to keep their attention on her and Lionel so they wouldn't look out the window. All they had to do was stay on the side of the short table. "Where are the papers?" she asked.

Lionel was looking up at her with shocked, hurt eyes. "I'm not signing any papers, Aileen," he said in a low voice. "I refuse to sign papers to give them anything that belongs to me."

Aileen squeezed his shoulders, giving him a reassuring look. "It's going to be okay, Lionel. We won't need that money. They can have a little bit of it, don't you think?" She tried to send him her thoughts, to let him know she didn't mean what she was saying.

He looked like he was going to cry. She shook her head and put one finger up to her lips.

"There's no need to worry. We're going to be just fine. Just fine. Don't worry." She continued with the same words, using the most soothing voice she could muster.

"Enough of the coddling," Buster yelled out. He slapped a small stack of papers on the table. "Sign this. You don't need to read it. Just sign it."

Aileen looked down at the document, lifting up on her knees. She pretended to read through it while she manipulated the rope around her ankles to free them.

She looked up when the rope fell away, drew in a deep breath, and screamed at the top of her lungs.

The abrupt action frightened the brothers. Their eyes opened wide, and they drew back from her like she had suddenly been possessed by a demon.

At that moment, the door burst open, and men flooded into the room.

Aileen barely caught what happened next. It was four against two, and the evil brothers didn't back down. Buster ran directly at the Winchester brothers, who tackled him to the ground. He shrieked and then went silent.

At the same time, Conrad shrieked in anger, whipped the gun from his side, and began to shoot. Caught by surprise, fear pierced Aileen, and she screamed, throwing herself over Lionel when the return gunfire sent bullets in their direction.

"Stop," Donald yelled. "You'll hit Aileen or Lionel."

"Doesn't matter now anyway," Aileen heard Henry say. "They're both dead. This is a small cabin. It's not good to pick a fight in here if it's two on one with a total of six. And two more people in the place."

Aileen pulled up from Lionel and looked down at him. For a moment, she was afraid tackling him had killed him. But he opened one eye and peeked out at her. "Is it safe?"

She giggled, sitting back more. She held out a hand to him. "Yes, it's safe. They won't be bothering you anymore."

Lionel sat up and brushed off his long nightgown as if that was all it needed to be clean again. He turned his blue eyes to Aileen and leaned his head close, murmuring, "It's been a long time since I had a lady fall on top of me. I've been lucky enough to have that happen before. But I was a much younger man then."

Aileen laughed, swatting playfully at him.

"You are silly, Lionel. Come on. Let's go home."

"Yes, why don't we?" Donald said, drawing Aileen's attention. She smiled as he held out his hand to help her to her feet. He pulled her into his arms against his chest and kissed her forehead and her cheeks. He moved to the tip of her nose and then pressed his lips against hers.

Aileen's body lit up with tingles. She melted against him. His kiss was brief but passionate. She didn't want it to end but maybe in a remote cabin with two dead bodies on the floor wasn't the most romantic place to get her first kiss.

She vowed to remember the cabin for the kiss. Not the killing.

29

The next morning came way too soon. Aileen turned over in bed, looking at the clock hanging on the wall. It was nearly nine in the morning, much later than she usually got up. She could hear the sounds of the visiting family downstairs. It was likely the family had let her sleep, knowing what she'd been through the night before.

She got dressed and went down the stairs. She stood at the door to the dining room and looked at the children and their parents, talking, eating, socializing. There was so much love in that dining room. Aileen could feel it in the hallway.

Even Donald had shown up and was having a conversation with Nate over a cup of coffee.

Happiness filled her heart. She wanted Lionel to join in and decided to go up and get him.

His door was cracked a bit, which meant he'd already been up that morning, and it was all right to come in. For a moment, she thought he might already be in his study, but she looked out to the veranda and saw him sitting in his favorite chair out there.

She went through the room, noticing there was no breakfast tray on the table in front of him. She debated whether or not to go back and get one for him in case he didn't want to come downstairs.

But something stopped Aileen from leaving the room.

She stared at the top of his head, unmoving, only the tufts of his white hair drifting with the soft breeze.

Her breath caught in her throat.

"Lionel?" she said in a shaky voice.

He didn't move.

Tears came to her eyes, and she slowly walked to the glass double doors. She looked down at him from the side. His eyes were closed. His shoulders were slumped. His head was lying softly to the side.

She put one hand over her mouth and swallowed her tears.

"Lionel." She could only manage to whisper his name. She dropped to her knees by his side and took his hand in both of hers, pressing it against her wet cheek. "Not yet," she whispered, kissing the back of his hand. "Oh, not yet. Oh, Lionel. Dear, sweet man. Not yet." She lifted up on her knees and put her arms around his shoulders, laying her head on his shoulder. "Dear, dear, sweet man. I will never forget you. Goodbye, sweet Lionel. Goodbye."

AILEEN WATCHED the line of townsfolk moving past the casket. She'd seen many more people and many more tears than she'd been expecting at the funeral of Lionel McArthur. She had cried all the tears she had and could only look on in somber silence now.

Donald was at her side, holding onto her with his arm around her shoulders.

"I don't think he was as friendless as he thought he was," Donald murmured softly.

"I was thinking the same thing," Aileen replied, also keeping her voice low. She watched as a woman reached into the casket to lay a red rose on Lionel's chest. "But I don't think he thought he was friendless as much as he didn't want to burden anyone with the chaos those two brothers were threatening."

"And now we can have children that look like Lionel." He looked down at her with a gentle grin. "Just like he wanted."

"Yes, I think he got his way all around, wouldn't you say?" Aileen asked. "Other than dying, I mean." She felt a pang of guilt for making light of the situation. But she felt like Lionel would see the humor in it, too.

"What are you planning to do now?" he asked.

Aileen thought about the question. She wasn't sure exactly what he meant by it. She moved her eyes from the procession of people to his handsome face.

"Marry you? Live my life? Have some children?"

He chuckled. "I meant with the business. You aren't planning to sell us all out, are you?"

"What would even make you ask me something like that?" Aileen demanded, a little more harshly than she meant. She was at the funeral of her "husband", now a very wealthy widow, and he was asking her if she was going to sell the ranch. She shook her head.

"You aren't thinking straight, Donald. Of course I'm keeping the ranch. You can buy out Henry's share if he wants to build a place of his own. Has he ever considered that?"

Donald turned her to him, making her look up at him. "Look at you. Worried about Henry and his family now. You are such a nice person. Did you know that? You care about everybody."

Aileen nodded. "I know. I really do. I can't help it. I try to be careful, but I end up trying to take care of everyone. I don't often do things for my own good." She grinned at him. "Until now, of course. Now I'm definitely doing something for myself."

"I love you, Aileen."

His abrupt confession stopped Aileen in her tracks. Her breath caught in her throat. He took her chin in between his fingers, brushing her skin gently instead of gripping it the way Buster had. She felt no pain when he touched her.

"Do you love me?"

Aileen was still in shock from having heard those words so abruptly. "I do love you," she said breathlessly. "I love you more than I've ever loved anyone in my life."

Donald paused before he spoke again, but he never took his eyes from hers. "Does that mean you will marry me and make me the happiest man alive?"

Aileen felt all the blood drain to her feet. Her knees almost buckled, but she held onto him, keeping herself standing.

"I will marry you," she whispered. "I want to have a family with you and live here on the ranch with you for the rest of my life." She lifted upward and pressed her lips against his. "I love you, Donald Ferris. I love you so much."

He kissed her and folded her in his arms, holding her tight. She couldn't believe how happy she was with him, how warm she felt, how much he loved her.

They walked side by side to the doors of the church. They would meet everyone at the cemetery, where Lionel would be laid to rest in a grave near his mother and father and his beloved Catherine.

Aileen looked up when the sky broke above her head, and rain began to pour. They were still under the church porch roof, so they weren't wet. The rain didn't help the melancholy mood that hung over the crowd of people there to mourn their friend's passing. The memorial service held before the funeral was somber. Hushed stories had made their way around the room, and Aileen had caught several of them. Neighbors and friends spoke of ways Lionel had helped them in the last decade or two. No one mentioned his previous behavior and ill-mannered ways.

Aileen was glad. She also didn't hear a peep about the deaths of Lionel's stepsons. She was grateful for that as well.

She would wait until the graveside service to throw her three yellow roses into the ground with her late husband. It pulled at her heartstrings, watching the men lower the casket into the hole they had dug for him.

Donald pulled her close to him. She rested her head on his chest, feeling a heavy sadness in her chest.

"It's gonna be all right, sweetheart," Donald whispered, kissing the top of her head and squeezing her. "You gave him what he wanted before he left this earth."

She looked up at him. "We both did. And I know he left us happier than he's been in a long time."

Donald lifted his eyebrows. "Like me."

She smiled softly. "And me."

The wedding between Aileen McArthur and Donald Ferris went off without a hitch. She'd told everyone ahead of time she wasn't going to give up Lionel's name. Donald offered to take her name, and she didn't see why there would be a problem with that, except that his family name would die off if he didn't use it, seeing as how his brothers had passed, and he had only sisters left.

He decided to use both and put a hyphen in between.

After the perfect ceremony, where Aileen felt she and Donald looked their absolute best, they all met in the grand ballroom of the McArthur Ranch for the reception. Irene had cooked up quite a lot of food to serve their guests, and Belle and Mary were two of the happiest serving girls Aileen had ever seen. Their smiles beamed as they took food and drink around to the people.

"This is a mighty fine shindig you have going on here, Mrs. Aileen," Henry said, coming over to her table and dropping in the chair to her left. "You and Donald should have plenty of parties. You'd make a lot of people in Gustaf's Corner real happy. Some of them probably remember coming here when it was a happy place, while Catherine was here, and Lionel was happy. Before the boys turned into complete scoundrels."

Aileen looked at her husband, feeling a little tingle at the thought that they were now officially married. "What do you think, Donald? Lots of parties? Lots of life in this house? We'll have to do it before we have a lot of kids. I'll be spending all my time running after them."

Donald grinned at her. "Parties are nice," he said, "but I won't mind not having many when we have kids. You never know. Maybe they will enjoy parties. I know plenty of kids who do."

Both Lionel and Aileen laughed. "The only parties I want after we have children are birthday parties, holiday parties, and when the Winchesters come from Shady Forks with all their kiddies. I'm sure it will be lots of fun."

"You've got a nice family there, Aileen," Henry said, lifting his glass and using it to gesture toward Nate and Theresa, who were in the middle of the floor dancing. The guitar player was strumming out a fast rhythm tune, and people were gathering in the middle of the floor to dance. "Look how happy they are."

Aileen watched her friends, a smile plastered to her face. By the end of the day, her cheeks were going to hurt.

"Everything is so wonderful," she whispered, scooting over to rest her body against her husband. He shifted in his seat to get comfortable, pushing his arm underneath her to hold her in place. He gave her a kiss on the top of her head.

She closed her eyes and smiled. She loved it when he did that.

Nate had given her away at the wedding ceremony, and Theresa had acted as her matron of honor. It was Henry who had stood up for Donald as his best man.

Aileen watched everyone dancing, her mind turning to sad thoughts. She missed Lionel. She'd grown close to him in the two weeks, or so she knew him. He'd started out with deception and ended up making her love him. She was glad he was buried so close by. She had already planned to go by his grave every Sunday and freshen it up, clean it, clear away leaves and snow on the off-seasons, plant flowers during the spring and summer.

"Donald."

Aileen came out of her thoughts and lifted her head to see two women heading for the table. She heard Donald groan.

"Who is that?" she asked.

"I didn't think they would come," Donald said in a low voice. He pushed up, forcing Aileen to sit up straight. She looked from Donald to the women, who were closing in fast.

"Donald. Look at you. I can't believe it. Look at you. Married."

The women gushed over him, and Aileen knew who they were without him having to introduce them. They didn't pay much attention to her. Both of them took turns placing Donald in a face hold with fingers that ended in long fingernails. They were both draped in jewelry, but Aileen had a sneaking feeling they weren't real gems.

Finally, the one closer to her let go of Donald

and looked at her. "You must be Aileen," she stated dramatically.

"Aileen." The other woman, not to be outdone, turned from her brother and swept over to take Aileen's face in her hands the way she'd done to Donald. "I am Suzie, my dear, and this is Sandy. We are Donald's sisters. I know he must have told you about us. I can't believe we haven't been here to see our dear brother in so long."

Aileen blinked rapidly, stunned into silence.

When they were done rubbing her face and telling her how beautiful she was, the two women turned back to their brother. Donald stood up abruptly before either of them could squeeze his face again. He was trying to be polite and smile at him, but Aileen could see him squirming.

She jumped in between the ladies and her man, smiling broadly at them.

"I hope you don't mind. Suzie. Sandy. I'm going to take my husband to the dance floor. You're free to join us if you'd like. There's plenty of room."

She dragged a grateful Donald onto the floor and joined the rest of her family, hopping around to the jaunty music being played.

She joined hands with Theresa and started a link-up all around until everyone was in a huge circle. It wasn't just the instruments that were making music. Everyone in the crowd was singing along as they hopped to the tune. They all flowed inward, joining up and lifting their hands as they closed in the circle. In the middle, they all cried out in joy. They danced backward, making the circle big again. When the circle was open, they repeated their joyous call and began to flow back inward.

As Aileen danced, she shed tears of happiness, squinting through her watery eyes, taking the happiness she saw around her. Her heart was filled with love.

She could never have asked for everything she'd been given. She didn't know what she'd done to deserve such happiness. She thanked God she decided to venture out on her own, despite her fears.

She now had exactly what she wanted.

A life of her own.

Click here for more Blythe Carver books!

Sign up for the newsletter to be notified of new releases.

Click on link for
Newsletter
or put this in your browser window:

landing.mailerlite.com/webforms/landing/p6l2s1